PRETENDER TO
THE THRONE

PRETENDER TO THE THRONE

BY

MAISEY YATES

To my readers.
This book exists because you asked for it.
And I'm so very glad you did!

CHAPTER ONE

"Either die or abdicate. I'm not particular about which one you choose, but you'd better make a decision, and quickly."

Alexander Drakos, heir to the throne of Kyonos, dissolute rake and frequent gambler, took a drag on his cigarette before putting it out in the ashtray and dropping his cards onto the velvet-covered table.

"I'm a little busy right now, Stavros," he said into his phone.

"Doing what? Throwing away your fortune and drinking yourself into a stupor?"

"Don't be an idiot. I don't drink when I gamble. I don't lose, either." He eyed the men sitting around the table and pushed a pile of chips into the pot.

"A shame. If you did, then maybe you would have had to come home a long time ago."

"Yeah, well, you haven't seemed to need me."

It was time for the cards to go down, and those who hadn't folded earlier on in the round put their hands face up.

Xander laughed and revealed his royal flush before leaning in and sweeping the chips into his stack. "I'm cashing out," he said, standing and putting his chips into a velvet bag. "Enjoy your evening." He took his black suit jacket off the back of the chair and slung it over his shoulder.

He passed a casino employee and dropped the bag into the man's hands. "I know how much is in there. Cash me out. Five percent for you, no more."

He stopped at the bar. "Scotch. Neat."

"I thought you didn't drink while you gambled," his brother said.

"I'm not gambling anymore." The bartender pushed the glass his way and Xander knocked it back before continuing out of the building and onto one of Monaco's crowded streets.

Strange. The alcohol barely burned anymore. It didn't make him feel good, either. Stupid alcohol.

"Where are you?"

"Monaco. Yesterday I was in France. I think that was yesterday. It all sort of blurs together, you know?"

"You make me feel old, Xander, and I am your younger brother."

"You sound old, Stavros."

"Yes, well, I didn't have the luxury of running out on my responsibilities. That was your course of action and that meant someone had to stay behind and be a grown-up."

He remembered well what had happened the day he'd taken that luxury. Running out on his responsibilities, as Stavros called it.

You killed her. This is your fault. You've stolen something from this country, from me. You can never replace it. I will never forgive you.

Damn.

Now that that memory had surfaced another shot or four would be required.

"I'm sure the people will build a statue in your honor someday and it will all be worth it," Xander said.

"I didn't call to engage in small talk with you. I would rather strangle myself with my own necktie."

Xander stopped walking, ignoring the woman who ran into him thanks to his sudden action. "What did you call about then?"

"Dad had a stroke. It's very likely he's dying. And you are the next in line for the throne. Unless you abdicate, and I mean really, finally, abdicate. Or you know, chain a concrete ball to your neck and hurl yourself into the sea, I won't mourn you."

"I would think you'd be happy for me to abdicate," Xander said, ignoring the tightness in his chest. He hated death. Hated its suddenness. Its lack of discrimination.

If death had any courtesy at all, it would have come for him a long time ago. Hell, he'd been baiting it for years.

Instead, it went after the lovely and needed. The ones who actually made a difference to the world rather than those who left nothing but brimstone and scorch marks in their wake.

"I have no desire to be king, but make no mistake, I will. The issue, of course, lies in the production of heirs. As happy as Jessica and I are with our children, they are not eligible to take the throne. Adoption is good enough for us, but not sufficient per the laws of Kyonos."

"That leaves…Eva."

"Yes," Stavros said. "It does. And if you hadn't heard, she is pregnant."

"And how does she feel? About her child being the heir?"

"She hates it. She and Mak don't even live in Kyonos and they'd have to uproot their lives so their child could be raised in the palace, so he or she could learn their duty. It would change everything. It was never meant to be this way for her and you know it."

Xander closed his eyes and pictured his wild, dark-haired sister. Yes, she would hate it. Because she'd always hated royal protocol. As he had.

He'd taken her mother from her. Could he rob her of the rest of her dreams, too?

"Whatever you decide, Xander, decide quickly. I would ask that you do so in two days' time," Stavros continued, "but if you want my opinion…"

"I don't." He hung the phone up and stuffed it into his pocket.

Then he walked toward the dock. And he wondered where he might find a concrete ball.

Layna Xenakos dismounted and patted her horse on the neck. Layna was sweaty and sticky, and the simple, long-sleeved shift she was wearing didn't do very much to diffuse the heat.

But she was smiling. Riding always did that for her. Up here, the view of the sea was intoxicating, the sharp, salty ocean breeze tangling with the fresh mountain air, a stark and bright combination she'd never experienced anywhere else.

It was one of the many things she liked about living at the convent. It was secluded. Separate. And here, at least, lack of vanity was a virtue. A virtue Layna didn't have to strive for. Vanity, in her case, would be laughable.

She pulled her head scarf out of her bag and wound her hair up, putting everything back in place. The only thing she could possibly feel any vanity about—her hair—safely covered again.

"Come on, Phineas," she said to the horse, leading the animal up to the stables and taking care of his tack and hooves before putting him in his stall and walking back out into the sunlight.

Technically, that had probably been a poor use of meditation time, but then, she rarely felt more connected to God, or to nature, than when she was riding. So, she imagined that had to count for something.

She walked toward the main building of the convent. Dinner would be served soon and she was hungry, since her afternoon's contemplation had been conducted on horseback.

She paused and looked over the garden wall, noticing tomatoes that were ready to be picked, and diverted herself, continuing on into the garden, humming something tunelessly as she went.

"Excuse me."

She froze when a man's voice pierced the relative silence. They interacted with men in the village often enough, but it was unusual for a man to come to the convent.

For a second, right before she turned, she experienced a brief moment of anxiety. Would he look at her like she was a monster? Would his face contort with horror? But before she turned fully, the fear had abated. God didn't care about her lack of outer beauty, and neither did she.

And moments like this were only a reminder that she did have to worry about vanity having a foothold. That it was an impediment to the service of others.

That, in a nutshell, was why she was a novice and not a sister, even after ten years at the convent.

"Can I help you?" The sun was shining on her

face, and she knew he could see her fully. All of her scars. The rough, damaged skin that had stolen her beauty. Beauty that had once been her most prized feature.

The sun also kept her from seeing him in detail. Which spared her from whatever his expression might be, whatever reaction he might be having to her wounds. He was tall, and he was wearing a suit. An expensive suit. Not a man from the village. A man who looked like he'd stepped out of the life she'd once lived.

A man who reminded her of string quartets, glittering ballrooms and a prince who would have been her husband. If only things had been different.

If only life hadn't crumbled around her feet.

"Possibly, Sister. Although, I'm doubting I'm in the right place."

"There isn't another convent on Kyonos, so it's unlikely."

"I find it strange I'm at a convent at all." He looked up, the sun backlighting him, obscuring his features. "At least, I find it strange I haven't been hit by a lightning bolt."

"That isn't really how God works."

He shrugged. "I'll have to take your word for it. God and I haven't spoken in years."

"It's never too late," she said. Because it seemed like the right thing to say. Something the abbess would say.

"Well, as it happens, I'm not looking for God. I'm looking for a woman."

"Nothing but Sisters here, I'm afraid," she said.

"Well, I'm led to believe that she is that, too. I'm looking for Layna Xenakos."

She froze, her heart seizing. "She doesn't go by that name anymore." And that was true, the sisters called her Magdalena. A reminder that she was changed, and that she lived for others now and not herself.

And then he started walking toward her, a vision from a dream, or a nightmare. The epitome of everything she'd spent the past fifteen years running from.

Xander Drakos. Heir to the throne of Kyonos. Legendary playboy. And the man she'd been promised to marry.

Quite literally the last man on earth she wanted to see.

"Why not?" he asked.

He didn't recognize her. And why would he? She'd been a girl last time they'd seen each other. She'd been eighteen. And she'd been beautiful.

"Maybe because she doesn't want people to find her," she said, bending down to pick tomatoes off the vine, trying to ignore him, trying to ignore her heart, which was pounding so hard she was certain he could hear it.

"She's not hard to find. Simple inquiries led me here."

"What do you want?" she asked. "What do you want with her?"

Xander looked at the petite woman, standing in the middle of the garden. She had mud on the hem of her long, simple dress, mud on the cuffs of her sleeves, too. Her hair was covered by a scarf, the color given away only by her eyebrows, which were finely arched and dark.

One side of her face showed smooth, golden skin, high cheekbones and a full mouth that turned up slightly at the corners. But that was only one half of her face. That was where her beauty ended. Because the other side, from her neck, across her cheeks and over the bridge of her nose, was marred. Rough and twisted, her lips nearly frozen on that side, too encumbered by scar tissue to form a smile. Not that she was smiling at him. Even if she were, though, he imagined that grimace was permanent, at least on that part of her face.

This was the sort of woman he expected to find up here. Not a giggling, glittery socialite like Layna. She'd practically been a girl when they'd been engaged—only eighteen, on her way to womanhood. And beautiful beyond belief. Golden eyes and skin, and honey-colored hair that had likely been lightened via a bottle. But whether or not it was natural hadn't mattered. It had been beautiful—shining waves of spun gold mingled with deep chocolate browns.

He'd known even then that she would make a perfect queen. What was more important was that she'd been loved by the people. And she came with wonderful connections, since her father had been one of the wealthiest government officials in Kyonos, much of his success derived from manufacturing companies based out of the country.

As far as he could tell since his return two days ago, the Xenakos family was no longer on the island. Except for Layna. And he needed to find her.

He needed her. She was the anchor to his past. His surest ally. For the press, for the people. They had loved her, they would love her again.

They would not, he feared, feel the same way about him.

"We have some old business to discuss."

"The women who live here don't want to discuss old business," she said, her voice trembling. "Women come here for a new start. And old...old anything is not welcome." She turned away from him, and started to walk into the main building. She was going to walk away from him without answering his questions.

No one walked away from him.

He started toward the garden, and blocked her path. She raised her face to him, her expression defiant, and his heart dropped into his stomach.

He hadn't realized. Of course he hadn't. But now that he could see her eyes, those unusual eyes, fringed with dark lashes, he knew exactly who she was.

She was Layna Xenakos, but without her beauty. Without the laughing eyes. Without the dimple in her right cheek. No, now there were only scars.

Not very much shocked him. He'd seen too

much. Done too much. He and the ugly side of life were well-acquainted. And he knew well that life's little surprises were always waiting to come and knock you in the teeth. But even with that, this wasn't anything he'd expected. Nothing he could have anticipated.

From the time he'd left Kyonos, he'd very purposefully avoided news regarding his home country. Only recently, when his sister had married her bodyguard and when Stavros had married his matchmaker, had he read articles concerning his homeland, or the royal family.

Because he hadn't been able to stop himself. Not then. But every time he opened the window on that part of his past, it was like scrubbing an open wound.

And it took a lot to wipe his mind and emotions free of it all again. A lot of drinking. A lot of women. Things that made him feel like a different man than the one he'd once thought he was, than the one he was trained to be. Things that created happiness. Before they created a gigantic headache.

One thing he'd never thought to look for had

been the fate of the woman he'd left behind. But obviously, something had happened.

"Layna," he said.

"No one calls me that," she said, her tone hard, her expression flat.

"I did."

"You do not now, your highness. You don't have that right. Do you even have the right to a title?"

That burned. Deeper than he'd imagined it could. Because she was edging close to a pain he'd rather forget.

"I do," he growled. "And I will continue to." His decision was made. Whether or not it made sense to anyone, including himself, his decision was made. He had come back, and he would stay. Though, no one knew it yet.

He'd felt compelled to come and see the state of things first. And then…and then he'd felt compelled to find Layna. Because if there was one thing he knew, it was that he had grown unsuitable to the task of ruling. And if he knew anything else, it was that no one was more suited to be queen than Layna.

He had thought it unlikely she would still be unmarried. He hadn't counted on her being both unmarried and at a convent, but he supposed it wasn't any less likely than what he'd been doing with his time for the past fifteen years.

No, he took that back. It was unlikely. Everything about this was unlikely. Layna Xenakos, the toast of Kyonosian society, renowned beauty and bubbly hostess, shut away in a convent, wearing a drab dress. With scars that made her mostly unrecognizable.

"I should like you to go," she said, walking toward him with purpose. He could tell she meant to go right on past him.

He stepped in front of her, blocking her way. She froze, those eyes, so familiar, like a shot straight out of the past, locked with his. "I would like for you to unhand me as well, then leave."

"So unhospitable, Sister, and to your future ruler."

"Hospitality is one thing, allowing a man to touch me as though he owns me is another thing entirely." She stepped away from him, her expression fierce. "You might rule the country, you might own the land, but you do *not* own me, or anyone else here."

"You belong to God now then, is that it?"

"Less worrisome than belonging to you."

"You did once."

She shook her head. "I never did."

"You wore my ring."

"But we hadn't taken vows yet. And you left."

"I let you keep the ring," he said, looking down at her hands and noticing they were bare.

"An engagement ring isn't very useful when there is no fiancé attached to it. And anyway, I've changed. My life has changed. I suppose you thought you could come back here and pick up where we left off."

He had. And why not? It would be the story of the decade. The heir's return and his reunion with the woman the nation had always been so fond of. Except, for some reason, a very large part of him had assumed she'd simply been here in Kyonos, frozen in time, waiting for his return.

A large part of him had assumed that all of Kyonos had done so. But he had been mistaken.

There were casinos now. An electric strip by the beach. His brother Stavros's doing. The old town had been renewed. No longer simply a quarter where old men sat and played chess, it was now a place for hipsters and artists to hang out and "be inspired" by the beach and the architecture.

His sister was not the same. Not a dark-haired, mischievous girl, but a woman now. Married and expecting a child. His brother had become a man, instead of a rail-thin teenage boy.

His father was old. And dying. His father...

And Layna Xenakos had joined a convent.

"I will be straight with you," he said. "I am not the favored son of the Drakos family."

She nodded once but remained silent, so he continued.

"But I have decided that I will rule. For the next generation even more than for this one."

"What do you mean?" she asked.

"Stavros's children cannot inherit. And that would leave my sister's child. The changes it would require...it was never her cross to bear. I have done a great many selfish things in my life, Layna, and I intend to keep doing many of them. But what I cannot do, when it comes down to it, is condemn my brother to a life he never wanted. Or give to my sister's child a responsibility it was never meant to take on." He had ruined things for his siblings already. Their childhoods had passed by while he was gone. Children who'd had no mother.

Especially Eva. She'd been so young then. It was unfair. He couldn't continue to hurt her. He *wouldn't*.

"You speak of the crown as though it's a poison cup," she said, her words muted.

"It is in many ways. But it is mine. And I have spent too many years trying to pass it off to others." Yes, his. As far as anyone knew, it was his. It was the expectation. What he had trained for until he was twenty-one.

The truth, was another matter. But it didn't change Stavros's reality. It didn't change Eva's.

It didn't change what had to be done.

"A conscience, Xander?" she asked, using his first name, the sound sending a shiver through him. A ripple of memory.

"I'm not so certain I'd go that far. Maybe a bit of forgotten honor bred into me. Thanks to all that royal blood," he said, his tone dripping sarcasm. "Imagine my disappointment when I realized I hadn't replaced it all with alcohol."

"A disappointment for many," she said. She sounded more like her old self now. He'd officially destroyed her serenity. Perhaps a lightning bolt would be in the offing after all.

"I'm sure. But I had thought there might be a way of softening the blow."

"And that is?"

"You," he said. "I'm going to need you, Layna."

CHAPTER TWO

LAYNA FELT LIKE the world had just inverted beneath her feet, and only the wooden gate was keeping her from folding. "Excuse me?"

"I need you."

"I can't imagine why you think that, but trust me, you don't."

"The people love you. They don't love me, Layna."

"The people love me?" she spat, anger rising in her, anger she always thought was dealt with. Until something came up and reminded her that it wasn't. Something small and insignificant, like catching sight of herself in the mirror. Or burning her finger when she was cooking. In this instance, it wasn't a small something. It was the ghost of fiancés past, talking about the people. The people who had loved her.

She'd made her peace with some of the people of Kyonos. She served them, after all, but she didn't feel the way she once had about them—confident that she had a country filled with adoring fans.

Quite the opposite.

"Yes," he said, his voice certain still, as though he hadn't heard the warning in her tone.

"The people," she said, "behaved more like animals after you left. Everything fell apart, but I assume you know that."

"I didn't watch the news after I left. A tiny island like Kyonos is fairly easy to ignore when you aren't on it. And when you're drunk headlines look a little blurry."

"So you don't know, then? You don't know that everything…everything went to hell? That companies pulled up stakes, stocks went down to nothing, thousands of people lost their jobs?"

"All because I left?"

"Surely you knew some of this."

"Some of it," he said, his voice clipped. "But there's a lot you can avoid when you're only sober for a couple hours a day."

"I wouldn't know."

"I imagine vice isn't so much your thing."

"No."

"So the economy collapsed and I'm to blame? That's the sum of it?"

She shrugged. "You. The death of the queen. The king's depression. It was an unhappy combination, and no one was confident in the state of things. People were angry."

She looked at him and she tried to find a place of serenity. Of strength. What happened to her wasn't a secret. It was in newspapers, online. It was widespread news. It was just hard to say out loud.

But you aren't going to show him that you care. You aren't going to be weak. It doesn't matter. Vanity. All is vanity.

"There were riots in the streets. In front of the homes of government officials, who were blamed for the economic crisis. There were different kinds of attacks made. Several attempts at…acid attacks. We were leaving our home when a man pushed up to the front and tried to throw a cup of acid onto my father. He stumbled, though, and the man missed. I was hit instead. I don't think I need to tell you where," she said, attempting to smile. Smiling could be difficult enough at the best of times since half of her mouth had trouble obeying that command, but when she didn't feel like smiling it was completely impossible.

But telling the story was easier when she imagined it was another girl. When she remembered what happened without remembering the pain.

She searched his face. She seemed to have succeeded in shocking him, which was something she hadn't imagined would be possible.

"So, I think it's fair to say maybe the people don't love me as much as you think they do." She pushed past him now, determined to put an end to this. To this strange bit of torment from the past.

He grabbed hold of her, his hand on her arm sending a rush of heat through her. She breathed in sharply, his scent hitting her, like a punch in the chest.

Her head was swimming. With glittering palaces and silk dresses. Dancing in a sparkling ballroom in a man's warm embrace. A trip to the garden where his lips almost touched hers. Her full, beautiful lips, unencumbered by scar tissue. It would have been her first kiss. And right then she wanted to weep for the loss of it because now there would never be one.

Not on those lips. They were gone forever.

Not even on the lips she had now. Because she had vowed to never know that pleasure of life. To forego it in favor of serving others, and release her hold on her own needs. Not that it should matter. No man would ever want to kiss her anyway.

But Xander was…he was too much. He was here, right when she didn't want him, and not fifteen years ago when she'd needed him.

Right now, she didn't need him. She needed distance. The more Xander filled up her vision, the more faded everything else seemed to become. Xander was a look into a life that she didn't have anymore. Couldn't have. Didn't want.

She just needed him gone. So that she could start to forget again.

"I suppose you should go now," she said. "Now that you know how it is. If you're looking for a ticket to salvation, Xander, I'm not it."

"I'm not interested in salvation," he said. "But I do want to do the right thing. Novel, isn't it?"

"Well, I can't help you. Perhaps it's best you found your way back to the village."

"I'm staying here tonight."

"What?" she asked, shock lancing her.

"I spoke to the abbess, and explained the situation. I don't want the public knowing I'm here yet, not until I'm ready. And I intend to bring you with me."

"I see. And nothing of what I said matters?"

He shook his head, his jaw tight. "No."

"The fact that I'm not me anymore doesn't matter?"

He studied her face, the cold assessment saying more than any insult could. Before the attack, men…Xander…had never looked at her with ice in their eyes. There had always been heat.

"I'll let you know in the morning."

He turned and walked away from her, into the main building. She waited out in the yard, cursing silently and not caring that it was a sin as she stood there, hoping he was putting enough distance between them that she wouldn't run into him again.

She would speak to the abbess tonight and in the morning, hopefully Xander would leave. And he would go back to being a memory she tried not to have.

It was early the next morning when Mother Maria-Francesca called her into her office.

"You should go with him."

"I can't," Layna said, stepping back. "I don't want to go back to that life. I want to be here."

"He only wants you to help him get established. And as you want to serve, I think it would be good for you to serve in this way."

"Alone. With a man."

"If I have to concern myself with how you would behave alone with a man then perhaps this isn't your calling."

It wasn't spoken in anger or in condemnation, just as a simple, quiet fact that settled in the room and made Layna feel hideously exposed. As though her motives—motives she'd often feared were less than wholly pure—were laid out before the woman she considered her spiritual superior in every way.

All that ugly fear and insecurity. Her vanity. Her anger. And old desires that never seemed to fully die. Just sitting there for anyone to see.

"It isn't that," Layna said. "I mean, I'm not afraid of falling into temptation." And even less worried about Xander falling into temptation with her. "It's just that appearances..."

"Are what men look at, my dear. But God sees

the heart. So what does it matter what people might think? Of the arrangement, or of you?"

Such a simple perspective. And one of the main reasons she felt so at home here. But that didn't mean her ease and tranquility transferred to every place she went.

"I suppose it doesn't matter." And what she wanted certainly wouldn't come into play. She could hardly throw herself on the ground and say she didn't want to. Of course she didn't. True sacrifice was hard. Serving others could be hard. Neither were excuses she would accept.

"This is an opportunity to do the sort of good that most of us never get the chance to do. You have the ear of a king, in heaven and now on earth. You must use this chance."

"I'll…think about it. Pray…about it." Layna blinked back tears as she walked out of the room. By the time she'd hit the hall, she was running. Out the door and to the stables.

She couldn't breathe. She couldn't think. She needed to ride.

And she did. Until the wind stung her eyes. Until she couldn't tell if it was the burn from the air that made tears stream down her face, or the deep well of emotion that had been opened up inside of her. Threatening to pull her in and drown her.

She rode up to the top of the hill, the highest point that was easily accessible, and looked down at the waves, crashing below, against the rocks. That was how she felt. Like the waves were beating her against stone. Breaking her down.

Like life was asking too much of her. When she'd already given everything she had.

She leaned forward and buried her face in Phineas's neck. Maria-Francesca was right. It hurt to admit it. Even in her own mind, it hurt to admit it. She'd never taken her vows. And so much of that was down to herself.

Was down to that piece of her that missed the ballrooms. That longed for a husband. For children. For the life she'd left behind.

If she stayed here, she would be safe. But she would be stuck. She would never take her vows. Because it wasn't her calling. And she'd been too afraid to admit it for so long because she didn't know where else to go.

You can go with him.

Not for him. For her. For closure. So that the

ache she felt when she thought of Xander, and warm nights in a palace garden, would finally fade.

As it was, he'd been gone from her life with no warning. A wound that had cut swift and deep. An abandonment that had become all the more painful after her attack.

It was safe here at the convent. But it was stagnant. And she saw now, for the first time, that it shielded her, instead of healing her.

She could do this. She would do it. And when it was over…maybe something inside of her would be changed. Maybe she would find the transformation she ached for.

Maybe then…maybe then she would come back here and find more than a hiding place. Maybe then, she would be changed enough to take the final step. To take her vows.

Maybe if she finished this, she could finally find her place.

All of her belongings fit into one suitcase. When you didn't need hair products, makeup, or anything beyond bare essentials to wear, life was pretty simple. And portable, it turned out.

She shifted, standing in the doorway, looking at Xander, who had his focus on the view of the sea. "I suppose you have an ostentatious car ready to whisk us back to civilization?"

Xander turned and smiled, his eyes assessing. She didn't like that. Didn't like how hard he looked at her. She preferred very much to be invisible.

"Naturally," he said. "It's essentially an eight-cylinder phallus."

"Compensation for your shortcomings?"

The words escaped her lips before she even processed them. They were a stranger's words. A stranger's voice. One from the past.

So weird. Being with him resurrected more than just memories, it seemed to bring out old tendencies. In her life at the convent, sarcasm and smart replies were not well-received. But when she'd been one of the many socialites buzzing around Xander, wanting to catch his attention, when she'd moved in such a sparkling and sometimes cutthroat circle, it had been the best way to communicate.

They had all been like that. Pretending to be so bored by their surroundings, showing their cool with cutting remarks and brittle laughter. It struck her then that Xander had changed, too. He hadn't joined a convent, but he lacked the air of the smug aristocrat he used to carry himself with.

He still had that lazy smile, that wicked mouth. But beneath the glitter in his eyes, she sensed something deeper now. Something dark. Something that made her stomach clench and her heart pound.

"I apologize," she said. "That was neither gracious nor appropriate. I'm ready to go."

He shrugged and took her suitcase from her, starting to walk across the expanse of green. She followed him, over the hill and to the lot where a red sports car was parked.

"I'm a cliché," he said. "The playboy prince. It would be embarrassing if it weren't so much fun."

"There's more to life than fun."

"But fun is a part of it," he countered.

"Certainly."

He deposited her suitcase in the trunk of the car. "I think you might have forgotten the fun part," he said.

"You have that covered for the both of us, I

think." She moved her hand in a wide sweep, like she was presenting the car on a game show.

He smiled. "You have no idea."

For some reason that smile, that statement, made her stomach tight. "I imagine I don't."

"Why don't you get in the car and we can continue this while we head back down to Thysius?"

She hadn't been to the capitol in a couple of years, and just the thought of it filled her with dread. "What exactly are we doing?"

"Get in the car."

Fear wrapped its fingers around her throat, the desire to turn and run almost overwhelming. But she didn't. "Not yet. Where are we staying? What are we going to do?"

"The palace," he said. "You're familiar with it."

"Yes." Much too familiar. There was a time when it would have been her home. When she would have been the queen. Memories that seemed like they belonged in another life were crowding in, trying to remind her of all the things she'd tried so hard to let go of.

"The press will think it's all sensational." He opened his door and got inside and she stood outside, looking at her warped reflection in the slightly rounded window.

"That's what I'm afraid of." She pulled the car door open and got inside, closing it behind her.

The leather interior smelled new. And an awful lot like money. Such a strange contrast to the old stone walls of the convent. When he turned the key and the engine roared to life she couldn't help but think it was a very strange contrast. The pristine newness. The noise. So different than the ancient quiet she'd lived in for so long.

"This is the story that I need. You and me, collaborating on bringing the country into a new era."

"Why do I feel a bit like you just told me together we will rule the galaxy as father and son…."

"Are you saying I'm asking you to join the Dark Side?"

"I feel like it."

"Seems a strange reference for a nun."

"I'm not a nun, actually. Not yet. I'm a novice." And she had been for a near record amount of time. Speaking of movies, her life was becoming a bit *"How do you solve a problem like Maria."*

"And I do watch movies," she said. "There isn't a lot that happens up here, and we aren't all serious all the time."

He pulled out of the parking area and onto the road. And she wasn't "here" anymore, either. She was leaving. Heading into the world. Away from the convent, away from the village. Into the city. Toward people. And the press.

Panic clawed at her, a desperate beast trying to escape. But she held it in. Did she pray for serenity or was this part of her test? To do what she didn't want, for it to be hard. To have to persevere.

Suddenly, she just felt angry. She hadn't asked for any of this. Not for Xander to come back, not to have to be in the public eye again.

She hadn't asked to be attacked. To have her life stolen from her. And hadn't she taken it and turned it into something worthy? Why was she having to do this now?

Fear was doing its best to take her over completely. And its best was far too good for her taste. The farther she got from her home, the closer they drew to the capitol city, the more it grew.

She was shaking. A tremor that seemed to start from the inside and built outward until her teeth were chattering. She tightened her hands into fists, trying to will it to stop. But she didn't have the strength.

They took so much. He took so much. Don't let them have anything else.

That voice. That strong, quiet voice inside of her made the shaking stop. Because it was right. Too much of her pain belonged to Xander, to the people of Kyonos, and she wouldn't give them one bit more.

She would help. Help restore the nation, get it all back on track, get Xander into a good position. But she wouldn't give of herself. Her actions, her presence, yes. But nothing of her.

"It isn't just you," he said, his voice rough.

"What?"

"You aren't the only one who will be judged."

He was so in tune with her train of thought that she was almost afraid she'd voiced her fears out loud. "Maybe not. But I'm the only one of us who didn't earn the judgment."

It was true, even if it was unkind. So, okay, maybe she wasn't holding back all of herself from Xander. She was letting him have some of her anger.

He laughed and the car engine roared louder, the cypress trees outside the window turning into an indistinct blur of green as he accelerated. "Very true. I did earn mine. And I had a hell of a lot of fun doing it."

CHAPTER THREE

XANDER FELT LIKE he sometimes did after a night of heavy drinking. His head hurt. His stomach was unsettled. And memories pushed at the edges of his mind, threatening to crowd into the fore-front.

Yes, it was just like the aftermath of being drunk. Or being hungover was a bit like coming home.

He paused the car at the gate. Stavros didn't know he was coming. It had been a phone call he hadn't been certain he could make. Stavros might bring up the option of hurling himself into the sea again and he might end up taking him up on it. Instead of returning to this.

He picked his phone up and dialed Stavros's number.

"Are you at the palace?" Xander asked when he heard an answer on the other end.

"I am not." Stavros's response was measured.

"Where are you then?"

"Vacation. My wife wanted to go to Greece and my children are enjoying a slight change of pace. Palace life is quite boring to them, I fear."

"I do remember the drudgery," he said, looking up at the turrets, bright white against a sun-bleached sky.

And he was walking back into it. Back into the past. Suddenly, he couldn't breathe.

He wanted to run again in that moment. Because he could remember what had pushed him to it now, all too easily.

Blood. Death. Blame.

So much easier to run. To wrap himself in life's pleasures and ignore the pain.

"I can't imagine anything ever felt like drudgery to you. You never took it seriously enough."

"Maybe not then. But I'm here now. Oh, yes, I've decided to come back and assume the throne, I don't believe I mentioned that."

There was a long pause. He looked across the car at Layna, who was sitting there looking straight ahead, as though she was pretending she couldn't hear.

"I'm glad," Stavros said, at last, and Xander believed him. "But if this is a game to you, then I suggest you take your ass back to wherever you came from. It's been my life's work to bring Kyonos back from the brink, and I'll not have you destroy it."

"Don't worry, Stavros, I've only ever been interested in destroying myself."

"And yet, somehow, you seem to destroy others in the process."

Xander looked at Layna and felt an uncomfortable pang in his gut. "Not this time," he said. "Now, call and have them admit me, please."

"You'll find your quarters just as you left them."

He laughed. "I hope there's still porn under the mattress."

There was. Though it was hideously dated and nowhere near as scandalous as he'd imagined it to be when he was a young man only just starting down the path of debauchery.

The head of palace hospitality had ushered Layna to her room, and his father's advisor had walked him to his own quarters. The man, as old as the king, was blustering, shocked and trying to get answers from Xander who was, unfortunately for him, not in the mood to answer questions.

Instead he shut the man out, shut the door and looked around. That was when he found the magazines, just as he left them. They used to thrill him. He remembered it well. Now they just left him with this vague feeling of the stale familiar.

But then, life in general didn't thrill him much at this point. He'd seen too much. Done too much. He was less a carefree playboy than he was a jaded one. It was hard to show shock or emotion when one barely felt it anymore.

The glittering mystery had worn off life. Torn away the day his mother died. Forcing him to look at every ugly thing hidden behind the facade. And so he'd walked further into that part of life. The underbelly. Into all the things people wanted to revel in, but could never bring themselves to discard their morals—or their image—in order to do so.

But he'd done it. Morals didn't mean a thing to him. Neither did his image.

It was too hard to go on living in a beautiful farce when you knew that was all it was. So he never bothered. He was honest about what he wanted. He took what he wanted. As did those around him. Whether it was gambling, drugs or sex, it was done with a transparency, an unapologetic middle finger at life.

He'd found a strange relief in it. In being around all that sin in the open. Because it was the secrets, the pretense of civility, he couldn't handle.

And now he was back in the palace. Center stage for the show. Back in chains. Pretending to be someone he was never born to be.

He threw the magazines down onto the bed and looked around. He'd expected a few more ghosts. Or something. But he felt the same as he had before returning home.

Shame and regret were his second skin. They existed with him, over him. And so he'd spent his life reveling in the most shameful things imaginable. He would feel it either way. At least if he sought it out, it was his choice. Not something forced upon him by life.

Like standing beneath water that was too hot. Until you were scalded to the point where you didn't feel it anymore.

In truth, it had worked to a degree.

But only to a degree.

He pushed his hands through his hair and turned toward where his suitcases had been put. He would need ties, he supposed. He didn't wear ties. One of the things he'd cast off when he'd left Kyonos.

For now, he just had his suits and shirts he wore open-collared, but it would have to do. Just the thought of ties made it feel hard to breathe. Or maybe it was the palace in general.

Her pulled open the door to his room and stalked down the corridor, not sure where he was going. He grabbed the passing housekeeper. "Where is Layna?"

"Oh!" She looked completely shocked. "Your Highness…"

"Xander," he said. He had no patience for station and title. "Which room is she in?"

"Ms. Xenakos is in the east wing, in the Cream Suite."

"Great." He started in that direction. Because there was nothing else to do. There was no one else in the palace he wanted to talk to.

He wasn't certain why that was. He should seek out his father's major domo. He should go and see his father, who was in the hospital. He should call his sister.

He didn't do any of those things. He just walked through the expansive corridors, past open-mouthed palace staff, and toward the Cream Suite. He got lost. Twice. It was an embarrassment, but he just kept going until he got his bearings again.

Then he pushed open the heavy wooden doors without knocking, and saw Layna, sitting on the edge of the bed. Her face snapped up, and again, he was shocked by her appearance.

It hit him like a slug to the gut. She had been so beautiful. So many beautiful things had been destroyed in that time. Either by his actions, or his very birth. The fault was bred into him, in many ways.

"What are you doing?"

"I'm here to speak to you. And to…escort you to dinner."

It had been a long time since he'd escorted a woman to dinner. Usually he had sex with them, then they ordered room service and ate it naked. Although, on a good night, he kicked the woman out quickly, then ate room service by himself.

She blinked. "Escort me to dinner? Where?"

"Here will do. The staff has been alerted to my presence, and I have no doubt they're eager to welcome me back with my favorite food," he said, his tone dry. "Or at the very least they won't let me starve."

"I don't suppose the heir is of much use to anyone if he's starved to death. I also don't suppose he's much use to anyone if he's absent and drunk."

"No, it doesn't seem that I've done any good during my time away," he said, his voice tight. "But I'm not sure what I could have done here, either. I was not the king then. I am not now. I'm simply in line."

"But you left us," she said, a note in her voice, so sad, so fierce, he felt it in his bones.

"I left you," he said.

"Yes."

"Did I break your heart, Layna?"

She shook her head slowly. "Not in the way you mean. I didn't love you, Xander. I was infatuated, surely, but we didn't truly know each other. You were very handsome, and I can't deny being drawn to you. I'm a bit of a magpie for shiny things, you know."

"I was shiny?"

"Yes. The shiniest prize out there."

"Not sure how I feel about that."

"You'll live." She looked down. "I loved the idea of being queen. I was raised for it, after all."

"Yes, you were." He didn't have to say that he hadn't been in love with her. That much had been obvious by his actions. When he'd left Kyonos he'd hardly spared a thought for what it would mean to Layna. He hadn't been able to spare a thought for anything but his own pain.

"But I thought I would find someone else. Maybe Stavros."

"You wanted to marry Stavros?"

She shrugged. "I would have. But then... Then the attack happened and I didn't especially want to see anyone much less marry anyone."

"So you joined a convent? Seems extreme."

"No. I spent years struggling with depression, actually, but thank you for your rather blithe commentary on my pain."

That shocked him into silence, which was a rare and difficult thing. He didn't shock easily. Or, as a rule, at all.

"When did you join?"

"Ten years ago. I was tired of muddling through. And I saw a chance to make myself useful. I couldn't fit back into the life I had been in, so it was time to make a new one."

"And you've been happy?"

"Content."

"Not happy?"

"Happiness is a temporary thing, Xander. Fleeting. An emotion like any other. I would rather exist in contentment."

He laughed. "Funny. I don't think I've been happy. Not content, either. I like to chase intense bursts of euphoria."

"And have you managed to catch them?" she asked, her voice tight.

"Yeah," he said, shoving his hands in his pockets and leaning against the doorjamb, "I have. But let me tell you, the highs might be high…the comedowns are a bitch."

"I wouldn't know. I strive for a more simple and useful existence."

"Do you want to dress for dinner?"

She looked down at the simple, shapeless dress she was wearing. It was blue and flowered, the sweater she had over it navy and button-down, hanging open and concealing her curves entirely, whatever those curves might look like. "What's wrong with this?"

"Really?"

"I'm not exactly given to materialism these days, and unless you were dead set on looking at my figure," she said dryly, as though it were the most ridiculous thing on the planet, "I fail to see why you should be disappointed. I'm clean, my clothing is serviceable. I don't know what more you could possibly need from me. If I am to be an accessory in your attempt at being seen by your people as palatable, then I'm sure my more conservative style could be to your advantage."

"I don't think that was what people liked about you."

"Perhaps not, but it can't be helped," she said, her voice tart.

She bowed her head, brown hair falling forward. "You used to sparkle," he said, not sure where the words came from, or why he'd voiced them.

She looked up at him, fire burning in her golden eyes. "And I used to be beautiful. Things change."

He pushed away from the door, and images from the past fifteen years—the casinos, the women—

rolled through his mind. "Yes, they do. I'll see you at dinner."

He turned and walked out of the room, back down the corridor. And he got lost again on the way back to his room.

This damned palace was never going to feel like home. But he'd been a lot of places in the past fifteen years and none of them felt like home, either.

He was starting to believe it was a place that simply didn't exist for him.

CHAPTER FOUR

HE'D MADE HER feel self-conscious about her dress. More than that, his words had sliced through her like a knife, hitting her square in a heart she'd assumed would be invulnerable to such things.

I used to be beautiful. Things change.

Yes, they certainly did.

She was realistic about the situation with her face. Fifteen years of living with it, and there was no other option. It had been hard. She'd been a woman defined by her looks, by her position in the public eye, and in one moment, it had all changed.

She was still a woman defined by her looks. But people didn't like what they saw.

The press called her disfigured. The former beauty. The walking dead.

Going out into the town had meant a chance she'd get her photo taken, and that meant a chance she'd appear in the news the next day.

It had driven her deeper into her own darkness.

Into isolation. It had been hell. And she'd had to escape.

Finding a way to a new life had been the hardest thing she'd ever done. Her family hadn't known what to do with her, they hadn't known how to help her. Their existence had been shaken, too. Their promised position as in-laws to the royal family vanished.

In the end, they'd all moved to Greece. Her mother, father and sisters. But Layna had stayed. And what she'd weathered should have made her immune to things like Xander's comments.

She was thirty-three. She wasn't a child. She knew now that life wasn't defined by dresses, balls and beauty. She did know it. So curse Xander for making her feel insecure. For making her feel like she should make an effort to look pretty when she met him for dinner.

Those things, they didn't matter. She had changed, and at the end of the day, she liked herself better now. At least now she didn't think the only way to live was by shopping the day away before going to a ball and pretending to be bored by all of it.

In some ways, she had more freedom now. If

something made her feel joy, she had no problem showing it. Her face made it impossible for her to blend in, impossible for people to do anything but judge her. So why worry about trying to seem cool and unaffected? There was no reason at all.

"I'm glad you could make it."

Layna paused at the entrance to the grand dining room. Another unholy mash-up between her life then and now. The expansive banquet table held no one but Xander. In the past, there would have been fifty dignitaries in attendance. And Layna would have worn her best dress. Xander would have worn a tie. They would have sat beside each other.

He was wearing a black suit jacket and a crisp white shirt open at the collar, revealing a wedge of golden skin and a dark dusting of hair.

She tried to remember if he'd had chest hair during their engagement. He certainly hadn't been as broad or muscular. He'd been lean. Soft-faced and handsome.

His face was more angular now, his jaw more pronounced thanks to the black stubble there. And his eyes, those eyes were so much sharper.

He was a man now.

"I'm not late," she said, walking slowly into the room. She wasn't sure if she should walk up to where he was, at the head of the table, and sit near him or not.

"No, but I was still wondering if you would bother to join me."

"I said I would. So I did."

"You aren't a soft girl, are you, Layna?"

"Have I ever been, Xander?"

A half smile curved his lips and it sent a strange, tightening sensation through her stomach. "No. Now that you mention it, you never were. Though you used to look like you might be."

"All that blond hair dye and the pink gowns. I suspect it was deceiving."

"Maybe to some. I remember, though, standing out on the balcony with you while you looked at the other guests."

So did she. Making snide observations about how Lady So-and-so had worn that gown to a previous event, and how Madame Blah-blah-blah's hair looked like a bird had chosen to nest in it.

Yes, she'd had opinions on everyone's looks. Specifically their shortcomings. The irony of that still burned.

"Yes, well, I was young. I had a lot of growing up to do. And I've had a lot of years to do it."

"And have you?" He leaned back in his chair, an arm rested on the table, an insolent expression on his face.

"Of course."

"See, I thought you might be playing hide-and-seek."

She stiffened and walked toward his end of the table and sat down, leaving an empty place between them. "What about you?"

"That's certainly what I'm doing. But I've been found, and I am now 'it,' as they say. Means I have to face all this."

"You sound about as thrilled as a man facing the gallows."

Several servants entered with food on trays, laid out in front of them grandly, their glasses filled with wine.

"Are you permitted?" he asked.

She nodded. "Yes. So long as it's not to excess. And anyway, I haven't taken my vows yet, remember?"

He nodded slowly. "I do. That is significant."

"It is." The servants uncovered the platters and

began to dish portions of rice, quail and vegetables onto her plate. She was surprised by how hungry she was. She hadn't eaten all day and she hadn't felt it. Because she'd been too filled up with nerves to do much of anything but worry.

"Why haven't you?"

Her face heated. "I haven't been permitted to take them yet."

"So it isn't your choice?"

She shook her head. "No. I'm committed." She hesitated to say the words because they felt false somehow. Especially after her revelation just before she left the convent. That part of her still wanted something from this life. From this palace. From Xander. She pushed her doubts away. "I was miserable before I went to the convent. I had no idea what to do with myself, no idea what I was supposed to...do with my life. Everything changed for me after."

"After I left," he said.

The servants cleared the room and they were left alone in the vast dining area. Layna looked out the windows, into the darkness, trying to find a point to focus on, something to anchor her to earth. Something to make her feel like the world hadn't changed entirely in the past twelve hours.

It was night out. There were still stars. She was still breathing.

"After you left," she said. "And then after the attack."

"I didn't think of you when I left," he said.

She laughed, and she surprised herself with her own bitterness. She'd done nothing but think about him. Worry for him. Pine for him. She'd lied a bit when she'd said he hadn't broken her heart. As much as she didn't believe she'd truly been in love with him, she'd cared.

Her heart and her future had been bound up in him. He'd been the man she'd imagined going to bed with at night. The man she'd thought she would have children with. The man who would make her a queen.

And then he'd gone, and taken with him her dreams. Her purpose.

Followed closely by the attack that took so many other things…gaining traction again had been nearly impossible.

"I didn't imagine you had."

"It was easier not to. But now I want to know."

"It was your father who told me you'd gone," she said. "And he asked that I return the ring."

"Did he?" Xander asked, his voice soft, deadly sounding.

"Yes. It was part of the Drakos family crown jewels, I could hardly keep it."

"Well, I'm sure it was badly missed in that dusty cabinet they keep it all in," he said, his tone dry.

"Are you really offended on my behalf?" she said, her throat tightening, anger pouring through her, hot and fast. "A bit hypocritical since you were the one who left."

"My leaving had nothing to do with you."

"No, as you said, you never thought of me again."

"I did. I thought of you after. It's true that when I ran, I only thought of me, and I am sorry for that. But later, I thought of you. I couldn't have been a husband to you, not under those circumstances."

She took a bite of the rice and the rich flavor knocked out some of her anger. She did not eat food like this at the convent. Even considering the unfortunate nature of the conversation, the food was amazing. As was the wine.

She let silence fall between them while she enjoyed her meal. She made a mistake when she looked up, and her eyes caught his. And she couldn't look away. Everything in her went taut, her breath pausing, her heart slamming forward. All she could do was stare at him.

He was so familiar. A face she tried never to remember. That perfect golden skin, the dark brown eyes fringed with thick black lashes. Lips that promised heaven when he smiled, and made a woman imagine he could take her to a beautiful sort of hell with a kiss.

All of that was so familiar.

But the lines around his mouth were harder now. Marks by his eyes showed the ghosts of his smiles.

He had been beautiful at twenty-one. At thirty-six he was no less stunning.

Time had not been quite so kind to her. And anyway, she had absolutely no business looking at him like she was. No business memorizing the new lines on his face. It was like she'd been in a coma, and she was slowly waking up. Slowly seeing new things. Or, remembering old things. She didn't like it. She was starting to remember why she'd worked so hard to forget.

"I wasn't meant to be your wife," she said, looking back at her food.

"You don't think?"

"Clearly not. I found a new calling. The place I'm supposed to be."

"You think you're better off hiding in the mountains than you are as the queen of Kyonos?"

She'd always thought she would be a good queen. But with a girl's insight. She'd loved the idea of the status and power. That everyone else was so jealous of her for having caught Xander's eye, or, more honestly, the eye of his parents.

Now she understood it had been her father's merit more than her own that had earned her the consideration. At the time it hadn't mattered. She'd only thought how beautiful she would look wearing the crown.

But now, ironically, that the position was no longer on the table, she saw all the good she could do. All that needed to be done to fix her country.

Prince Stavros had done an admirable job with it, more than admirable, but there were still things to be done on a humanitarian level, and as someone who had done nothing but serve for the past ten years she was well familiar with what tasks needed to be tackled head-on.

Nice that she knew all that. Now that there was nothing she could do about it. That would be for the woman who married Xander. And that woman would not be her.

A twinge of anger hit her in the chest, burned like a pinprick and spread outward. This had been her future. And she was sitting in it now, not a part of it.

She looked back up and saw him watching her, and it hit her then. What she'd lost. They would have been married for nearly fifteen years by now. There would have been children. She wouldn't be scarred.

It did no good to dwell on the past. It did no good to turn over what-ifs. But it was so hard when your biggest what-if was sitting across from you eating dinner, like he might have done if you'd married him way back then.

Yes, it was a whole lot harder not to what-if in that situation. Easier when cloistered in a convent, away from any part of the life she'd once lived. Impossible here and now.

"I wasn't meant to be queen," she said, her tone strong, a sharp contrast to what she actually felt.

"Perhaps I wasn't meant to leave." His words burned through her. Because he had left. It didn't matter what should have happened, only what had.

"Why bother turning it over, Xander? It's what happened. You did leave. And things have changed. We didn't freeze in time here while you were gone like I'm sure you imagined we did. We went on. Things have happened, things that can't be undone. I would have been…a silly and self-ish princess back then anyway. And now…now it just couldn't be."

"It's hard not to turn it over here, though, isn't it?"

She put her palms flat on the table, her heart pounding, blood rushing through her ears. "Why did you come back? Really. I mean…what changed? You left, and no one ever thought you would be back, but here you are now, and you're dragging me into it, so I want to know why."

He shook his head, didn't say anything. He only stared out the windows into the darkness outside.

"Answer me, Xander," she said. "I have a right to know why you've crashed back into my life."

"Because there was nothing out there," he said. "No answers. It fixed nothing. If Stavros wanted the throne, if it didn't throw Eva's future into disarray, I would never have come back. But I don't do any good by being gone. I'm not sure I'll do much good being back. I'm not sure I'm even capable of doing good. I think that where I'm concerned, all of the bad might run too deep." When he said it like that, she believed he might be right. "But I came back, because if I didn't it would stay broken. And now that I'm here, it might all remain that way, but at least it's my broken mess and not theirs."

"You love them, don't you?"

"I don't love easily," he said, his voice rough. "But I would die for them."

"That's something."

"A sliver of humanity?"

"Yes," she said, taking a deep breath. "What am I doing here, Xander? You've given me a reason. The press. But I have to tell you, I'm not sure I believe it."

"It's part of it," he said.

"I need all of it."

"Do you want an honest answer?"

"If you know how to give one."

"I don't lie, Layna, it's the one sin I don't indulge in. Do you know why?"

She put her fork down. "I'm on the edge of my seat."

"Because people lie to protect themselves. To make people like them. To hide what they've done because they're ashamed. I have no shame, and I don't care if people like me. My sins are public property."

"Then give me an honest answer."

"I thought I might marry you," he said, his tone conversational, light. As though he'd mentioned that it was a clear night and the food was lovely, and not that he'd been considering asking her to be his wife.

"You did?" she asked, her lips numb, her entire body numb suddenly, from fingertips on down.

A wife. *Xander's* wife.

It was impossible. And she didn't want it anyway. Her life was in the convent, it was serving people and living simply. It was shunning the frivolous things in the world. Denying passions and finding contentment in the small things. In the things that were worthy.

It was this palace. This man. They washed those old memories in brilliant colors, where for years they'd always been faded.

And now she could see again, so clearly, how lovely it had all been. She could taste the excitement of it. That secret ache bloomed, flourished, let her dream. Let her see the glitter, the sparkle and what might be for one beautiful moment.

But it only lasted for a moment. Until a root of bitter anger rose up and choked out the bloom.

"Obviously," he continued, "that can't happen now."

She felt the sting of his words like a slap. "Obviously not. What would people think if you took me as a wife?"

"I only meant because you've chosen to forego marriage by joining a convent. Had I found you anywhere else I would have stuck to my original plan and proposed on the spot."

She bit down hard and tried not to say what she was thinking. Tried. And failed. "I would have told you to go to hell. On the spot," she said.

"You haven't changed as much as I initially thought."

She stood up. "That's where you're wrong. Everything's changed. I've changed, my whole life has changed."

He stood and started to walk toward her, dark eyes pinned to hers. "No, Layna, see I don't think you've changed as much as you think you have. When I look at you, I can so easily see the girl you were. You were blond then."

"Because I used to dye it."

"I suspected. But it did suit you."

"It's pointless vanity," she said, waving her hand.

"How is it pointless if you enjoy it? It can still be vanity, but it doesn't mean it's pointless."

"Yes it does. But make your point and be done."

He took another step toward her and her heart climbed up into her throat and lodged itself there. "You had fire. Beneath that airhead, mean-girl surface, you had more to you than anyone guessed. You were a little flame ready to become a wild fire."

She shook her head. "It doesn't matter. I've changed now and…"

"No. You're still doing it. You're still hiding who you are beneath something else. Beneath a shield.

The flame is still there, you just want to hide it. Up in the mountains."

"It's not my fire I'm hiding. It's my face. And if you want to pretend it doesn't matter then I'm going to tell you right now, Xander, no matter what you said before, you are a liar." Rage rattled through her, fueled her, spurred her on.

It hit her, as the force of it threatened to consume her, that of all the emotions she'd felt since her attack, she'd never been angry. Sad. Depressed. Lonely. She'd hit rock-bottom with those. Then she'd found a sort of steady tranquility in her existence at the convent.

But she'd never been angry.

Just now she was so furious she thought she might break apart with it. "Look at me," she said, "really look. Can you imagine me on newspapers and magazines? The face for our country? Can you imagine me trying to go to parties as if nothing had happened? Trying to continue on as if I was the same Layna as before? That's why I went to the convent. Because there it didn't matter if my face was different. There it's practically a virtue and here…here it's just not. I'm ugly, Xander, and whether or not I accept myself there will always be people who want to point it out. I've never seen a reason for putting myself through it."

He shoved his hands into his pockets, his eyes hard. "It will be commented on. I won't lie about that. But do you think people will resent your scars or my abandonment more?"

"Don't tell me you're honestly still considering me as queen material."

"I was very interested by the fact that you haven't yet taken your vows."

"My intent remains the same, whether or not I've taken final vows."

He reached out, took a piece of her hair between his thumb and forefinger. She froze. She hadn't been touched by a man in longer than she could remember. Male doctors were the last ones, she was certain. And then she hadn't registered the touch in any significant way.

But Xander had never been easy to ignore. Now, with his hand on her hair, just her hair, a flood of memories assaulted her. The catalog of moments when Xander had touched her in the past opened, forcing her to remember.

His hand over hers, or low on her back. An arm

around her waist. His warm palm on her cheek as his lips nearly brushed hers.

If they had married then, they would have kissed thousands of times by now. But as it was, they had never kissed once.

"But nothing is final," he said.

He lowered his hand, releasing her hair, and sanity flooded in a wave. She stepped back, blinking, that fresh and newfound anger coming to her rescue.

"Yes, Xander, everything is final. I have made my decision, like you made yours. I'll help you in any way I can, but don't insult me by pretending, even for a second, that you would consider making me your wife. Don't consider that I might allow it."

She turned and walked out of the room and when she hit the halls she suddenly realized that she was gasping for breath. She put a hand on her chest and blinked hard, fighting tears, fighting panic.

Xander was reaching into places inside of her no one had touched in so long, she'd forgotten they were there. Longings and regrets she'd buried beneath a mountain of all that lovely contentment she'd learned to cultivate from the sisters at the convent.

Xander made her restless. This palace made her remember. It made her want things....

She shook her head. No. She wouldn't let this happen. She wouldn't be shaken. She would help him. If only to help her country, her people.

But she wouldn't forget who she'd become. Who Xander's actions had forced her to become.

CHAPTER FIVE

XANDER UNBUTTONED HIS shirt and threw it onto the bed. He hadn't intended to bring up the marriage proposal like that. Hell, he hadn't meant to bring it up at all. She was a nun. Well, close enough to being one, anyway.

And then there were the scars. He couldn't pretend they didn't matter. She was right on that score. He needed a wife that would help improve his image in the public, and before he'd seen her, he'd imagined that she could do that. That their reunion would be seen as a true romance in the eyes of the media.

But how would they respond to a scarred princess? A princess who had been scarred during the turmoil caused by his leaving? A constant reminder of dark times for all of them. It had to be considered.

As for him, it didn't much matter. He would marry someone, he had to. But just because he had to marry didn't mean he had to be monogamous. He would be honest on that score with whomever he married, of course. But marriage was a necessity because he had to produce heirs, and preferably sooner rather than later. At thirty-six he was hardly getting any younger, and added to that, the people needed assurance that he could provide what was needed.

His plans were officially screwed.

Tomorrow, he was taking Layna to Kyonos's largest hospital, where he would make his first public appearance. And where he would be giving a sizable donation of his personal fortune, and making his intentions of ruling Kyonos known.

Because nothing eased the way like throwing charitable donations around. At least, he hoped it would ease the way.

The people loved Stavros. They wouldn't accept the change lightly. Come to think of it, he was sure it was why his brother remained out of the country, even knowing Xander was back. The bastard.

He nearly laughed out loud. No, Stavros wasn't the bastard here. He never had been. The bastard had always been him.

But it was too late to worry about that now. His decision was made.

He thought of Layna, of his need for a wife. Some of his decisions were made, but not all of them.

He would have to figure that part out as quickly as possible. Of course, in order to have it all figured out, he needed to know what he was dealing with.

He turned to his desk, to his laptop, sitting there, open. He typed in his name on the search engine and hit enter.

It had hit. The servants must have called. Someone had said something, because there were headlines already.

The Disgraced Heir's Return. He clicked the link and skimmed the article. It was filled with bile and innuendo. About all he'd done with his life since he'd been gone.

Prince Alexander Drakos, abandoned Kyonos like a rat when it was a sinking ship, saved, of course by Prince Stavros. All while Xander partied in Monaco, wasting his family fortune, sleeping with countless women while indulging in alcohol and illegal substances.

One source from an exclusive casino was quoted.

"One night, he was so drunk he could hardly stand straight. He put his arms around two women to brace himself and they helped him back to his room. I didn't see them leave until the next morning."
And this is the man who presumes to come back and be king of our great nation.

Xander closed the laptop, heat streaking up the back of his neck. He couldn't remember the night being referenced in the article, but he couldn't say it was a lie.

It wasn't going to be like he'd thought. It was going to be worse. And all he could do was go forward with the plan.

There was no other option.

"I assumed asking you to put on something more appropriate for the occasion would make you look at me like I'd grown a second head."

Layna was at the breakfast table, wearing an insipid pale pink shift and a sweater that was the color of a dirty rose. She looked up, her gaze serene. But it didn't cover the fire beneath. He'd spoken the truth to her last night. The fire was still there, fire she'd always been so desperate to hide. "I have no idea what you're talking about. My dress is the picture of appropriate."

"For a nunnery."

She arched a brow. "Funny that."

"You're not in the convent anymore, Dorothy."

"I don't suppose if I tapped my heels together three times I might find my way back."

"Unlikely. I doubt nuns are allowed to possess magic shoes."

"Novice."

"Either way," he said, crossing the room and planting his hands on the back of one of the dining chairs, "I am wearing a tie. And I don't think you understand just what a concession that is, so all things considered, perhaps you would allow me to get you a more appropriate dress for what I am certain will end up being a press conference."

Her expression went blank at the mention of the press. "What's the point? I'm not speaking in your press conference. I'm there to be your...what am I exactly—some homely, saintly representation of your good intentions? Or am I just supposed to stand close so that the lightning bolt you were concerned about earlier doesn't hit you?"

"I thought God didn't work that way."

She lifted a shoulder. "I said that before I'd spent this much time with you."

"I won't lie to you, you are here to give me a bit more of a savory appearance. And also because I think it lends nice closure to our story. If you can forgive me..."

"Oh, I see. Another layer to my usefulness." She stood, color slowly blooming in her cheeks as her voice rose. "You thought that if I would forgive you the country would follow suit. That if you came back and the woman you were engaged to before you left opened her arms to you, your people would do the same." And then she did something wholly unexpected. She started laughing.

Not just a giggle, but a laugh that seemed to take over her whole body. She put her hand on the back of the chair in front of her and doubled over, laughing so hard he thought she might choke.

"Oh, poor Xander," she gasped. "You came back

to find your queen, your key to your redemption and you found a scarred woman who'd given herself to the church. Your plans just aren't going well, are they?"

He wouldn't even mention the unflattering news pieces going around about him.

"You could say that," he said, his words clipped. He did not find the situation as funny as she did. But then, in his mind, none of this was terribly funny. It was all his worst nightmare as far as he was concerned.

He was back here, in the suffocating atmosphere of the palace, trying to pretend like he fit when he didn't. Trying to pretend the scars the past had left on him didn't hurt when they did. Trying to act like this was a future he was entitled to when he knew full well it wasn't.

But he was the only one who did know that. The only one who was still alive who knew it, anyway.

"Sorry I'm making it difficult for you to use me," she said, wiping her eyes. "I'm sure that must really mess things up."

"I thought you lived for the service of others."

"The poor and downtrodden, not entitled royal princes who don't know you can't find responsibility, honor or purpose in the bottom of a gin bottle."

He laughed, bitterness in the sound. "No, I know you can't, but that's not what I was looking for."

"What were you looking for?" she asked.

"I wasn't looking for anything. I was trying to lose something. Now are you ready to go or not?"

"I'm ready," she said, her eyes far too assessing for his liking.

"Fine then, let's go. And do your best to look saintly. If you can cultivate a halo on our way there I would really appreciate it."

Layna held her breath until she thought she would pass out. The press was already waiting at the hospital when they pulled up, so clearly someone on staff had leaked the news. It would be huge, of course it would. The heir to the throne back on Kyonos.

The implications were huge.

And all she could think about was that they would be taking her picture. That people would look at her.

Xander made her revert to a stupid, silly girl

who cared about insubstantial things. It was annoying beyond belief.

Just focus on all the good you can do with the kind of budget he has.

Yes, that was the key. She would direct him to the needs she knew existed. It would benefit Kyonos and it would benefit him. Everyone came out a winner. Having her picture in the paper was a small price to pay for doing that kind of good.

It really was. It didn't matter what they said. It didn't matter what they thought. Her body was just the place her soul lived, and the only beauty she had to be concerned with was the kind that was inside.

She repeated that, over and over again, but still when the car came to a stop and Xander got out, her hands started to shake.

They were taking pictures already. Xander's return would be the biggest news since his abandoning the island and it would be on every news station, in every paper.

He opened the limo door and before she could fully process her movements, she got out and was assaulted by a barrage of flashes and shouts. He took her arm and she kept her face tilted down as they walked into the hospital.

He released his hold on her when they were near the doors, then stood in front of her, the gesture oddly protective as he turned, addressing the press. "I will speak to you when we are done here. For now, my priority is to see how the most vulnerable of my country are getting on. I have brought with me an ambassador, one who knows the struggles of all of you. Please treat her with respect."

He turned back to the doors, his hand on her arm again as he led her into the hospital.

The hospital administrator was waiting for them and after making introductions it was clear Xander was waiting for her to lead things. "Is the hospital large enough to accommodate all of the patients that you need to see?" she asked.

"Prince Stavros has done an amazing job of building up our research center," the woman said. Her manner was reserved. Almost cold. She was trying to be friendly, especially since Xander was there to give money, but there was a brittleness there she wasn't hiding well. "As a result we're well-equipped in many areas, but yes, things are starting to feel understaffed, and the children's ward especially is very small. People travel here seeking treatment."

"A wonderful thing," Xander said, for the first time, his confidence sounding blunted. He knew when to tone himself down, which was a surprise to Layna, and a credit to him.

"Yes," Layna said. "What about emergency medical services?"

They finished the tour of the hospital, which included a trip through the cafeteria. Layna nearly laughed at Xander, trying to deal with a hospital version of a gyro. He was clearly not impressed.

"She was not thrilled to have me here, was she?" Xander asked as he took another bite of food.

"Not as much as one might have hoped," Layna said.

"Well, I imagined that's what I'll be contending with across the board. Stavros is well-liked. And I am not." He looked down at his meal. "I do have an idea of where we might increase the funding," he said, his voice low, only for Layna.

"Better idea, Xander, why don't you put some money aside to send the hospital cooks through a culinary course? Then they have transferable skills."

He paused, a half smile curving his lips. "This is why I brought you."

"I do have my uses," she said. "Even if I can't be made a queen."

He stared at her, for far too long in her opinion. It made her face hot, made her aware of her face. Annoying man.

"Are you ready to leave?" he asked. The hospital administrator had gone back to her office and they were standing in the lobby, staff and patients passing through. Some trying not to stare, some staring openly as they tried to decipher if the larger-than-life man standing there was a Drakos. If he was the long lost heir.

"Yes. As ready as I can be. I appreciated what you said to everyone before we came in. Hopefully they'll find it in them to be human. To both of us."

"Aren't you looking forward to the press ripping into me? They already have, you know."

She paused, waiting to feel some kind of relish at the thought, but she just didn't. "I actually don't want that. A surprise, I know. But I'm tired of this country feeling torn. I'm tired of grieving our losses. Tired of the unrest. Stavros has done an incredible job rebuilding, unifying, and the people love him. But there is a sense that everything isn't settled. That the royal family itself isn't healed. With the king so sick… Xander, I would rather you be accepted with open arms. And then I would like for you to take the people's trust and use it well, not abuse it. That's what I would like."

"And you want to go back up to your mountain then?"

"It's my years on the mountain that are helping you now. You have to admit, this wasn't your area of expertise."

"I've been a patient in hospital emergency rooms," he said, looking around them, "but I've been short on philanthropy in them."

"You have?" She was honestly shocked by that.

He laughed. "I've done no shortage of dumbass things in my time away, Layna. Just trust me on that. Too much speed in cars, too much drink, too much…everything." He paused. "Another advantage, I suppose to your being committed elsewhere. If you aren't my queen, you don't have to deal with my past."

"Is it so bad?"

He nodded slowly. "And there's a lot of it. Ready?"

She knew he was talking about facing the press. "Yes."

He walked out of the hospital and she followed slowly, dread filling her, her brain fuzzy, the world titled slightly.

"As has already been reported, in less than flattering words," he said, his voice loud, the microphones unnecessary, "I have returned, and I intend to take my place as heir to the throne. Of course, while my father is unwell, that doesn't mean it will happen now, or even in the next year, but I am here, and I'm here to stay. Layna Xenakos has graciously agreed to partner with me as I get familiarized with my home again. She's been living in service to this country, and she is the best choice, in my opinion, to show me where the greatest needs lie. If Layna can forgive me my choices, and welcome me back, I hope that her forgiveness is the start of my earning forgiveness from everyone. Though, I know that is a lot to ask. We all want what is best for the country.

If you can't trust me, at least, for now perhaps, we can stand united in that."

The air roared with questions as the press crushed in on them both. Xander took her hand and pulled her through the crowd. She tried to keep her head down, tried to keep them from being able to snap shots of the worst of her damaged face. Tried to let all of the questions blend into an indistinct blur so that she didn't hear any of them.

But she heard words. *Attack. Scars. Beauty. Ugly.*

She'd never spoken to the press after her attack, and neither had her family. There were so many unanswered questions for them. Between her and Xander the press had the most salacious bits of the past, right there before them, and they were rabid now.

"In the car," Xander said, opening the door. She obeyed and slid inside. He followed, slamming the door behind them. "Back to the palace," he said before putting the divider up between them and the driver.

He let out a rough breath and put his head back

on the seat. "Well, that went a bit better than anticipated."

"Did it?" she asked.

"They let me make a statement before mobbing us."

"Okay, yeah, there's that."

"It was better than they can be."

She looked at him. "How have you managed to avoid the press all these years?"

"Easy, actually. I don't go to places where they hang out. There will be no place to avoid them in Kyonos, but in the rest of Europe? In the States? No one cares. I made brief splashes in tabloids for the first couple of years. 'Dishonorable Heir Gambles Away His Fortune,' et cetera. But then people lost interest."

"I suppose it was the same for me. After the attack it was news. But they weren't allowed in the hospital to interview me. Then I was in too much pain to even consider talking to anyone. For a long time. I had a lot of surgeries." She didn't even like to say how many. "After that I didn't go anywhere. My parents moved to Greece where, you're right, no one cares about the drama that happened here, and I stayed on in their house with their servants for a while."

"Why didn't you leave?"

She frowned. "I…I was too tired." It was a terrible thing to admit. Even to remember. The depression had controlled her, not just emotionally, but physically. Breathing had often seemed too big of a trial. To move to Greece? It would have been unthinkable.

Those years were a haze, where she kept herself cradled by the gentle hands of painkillers that helped her sleep, helped her ignore the pain from her most recent surgery, and helped her live her days with blunted senses.

She preferred never to remember them. She'd come too far since then, and that place had been too dark. Although, there were times when it was important to remember it. It reminded her just how bright the sun was. How much better things were now.

Even sitting in the limo with Xander, with the press all but chasing the limo, it was better than that place. Because above all else, she had control now. She could leave if she chose. Could get up and walk away from Xander, from whatever she wanted to.

She had the power now. The energy and strength inside of herself to do it. She would never be stuck again.

"And has it been better here? Are you happy with your decision to stay?"

"It was terrible here, at first. That first five years…it was hell. The recovery was awful, Xander, I won't lie. It wouldn't have mattered where I was, not really. But when I got…well, when I got the worst, and I knew I had to figure out how to get better, it was right to change things as radically as I could. And that's why the convent was best for me. It's impossible to worry too much about your own drama when you have to confront what's happening with others."

"How did you connect with them?" he asked.

She looked down at her hands and smiled. "Some of the Sisters visited me in the hospital when I was recovering. And after every surgery. They checked on me sometimes. They cared. And they didn't look at me and see my scars. But they did see my pain, and they…cared."

"Your family?"

She sighed. "They didn't realize how bad it was. How bad it had gotten for me. Mainly because I lied to them. I told them I was fine when I wasn't and they wanted to believe I was telling the truth because it was so much easier. I don't blame them at all."

"Do you blame me?"

His words were stark in the silence of the car. Emotionless. He was asking, but he gave no indication that he cared either way.

"Yes," she said, and only realized just when she spoke the words that she meant them. That she did blame him, deep down, for the pain, for the isolation.

If he had stayed, at least she would have had a husband to stand by her. And maybe it would never have happened. Maybe the economy wouldn't have crashed, that she could never know. But she could have had someone.

She wouldn't have lost everything.

He nodded slowly. "I think that's fair. And I can handle having another sin added to the list."

"Do you think so?"

"Confession would take too long at this point,

Layna. I'm beyond it. I might as well just accept it for what it is and move on from there."

Her heart thundered, anger burning through her veins. "At least you can move on. Gloss over it, pretend it didn't happen. It's a lot harder to do that when you have to look at the effects of the past in the mirror every day."

"Then how about I wake up to the effects of the past every morning?"

"What?" she asked, her stomach hollowing out.

"I've changed my mind about changing my mind." He put his legs out straight in front of him, his eyes fixed ahead. "After thinking about it, I believe the best idea is for you to marry me."

CHAPTER SIX

SHE HAD BEEN silent the rest of the ride back the palace. He supposed that it was probably a no, but he wasn't going to let her get away with not giving an answer. In his mind, it just meant he had to change hers.

"I'm tired," she said, once they reached the entryway of the palace. "I'm going to my room."

"I shall accompany you."

"No, you shall not," she said, starting to walk away from him, down an empty corridor, away from where the servants were bustling around.

"Then we will speak here."

"No, we won't."

He went to stand in front of her and she stopped and backed up quickly, her back making contact with the wall. "Yes," he said, advancing on her. "We will."

He studied her face, really studied it, for the first time since that day at the convent. It was a shame what had been done to her beauty. She'd been uncommon. He could remember her clearly. Those full pink lips, smooth skin, perfectly arched brows. Oh, he had wanted her badly. He could still remember that.

Being twenty-one and wanting his fiancée with a ferocity that he could scarcely understand. He'd been no virgin, even then, but she'd made him feel like one. And his father had made it clear Xander wasn't allowed to touch her, at least not until closer to the wedding. Something about respect and honor. About preserving the people's vision of their future queen.

So he had obeyed.

But they never would have made it that long. The chemistry had been too potent.

He'd nearly kissed her once. He remembered because it had happened the day before his mother's death. The day before the revelation about who he really was.

After that, he hadn't seen her.

He lifted his hand and put his fingertips on her scar-roughened cheek, drawing them down her neck. He could imagine the attack clearly, how it had made these particular scars. A hard hit to her cheek, spray over her nose, eye and forehead, down one side of her neck.

The other side of her face was virtually untouched, but it made her scars all the more shocking. It gave them contrast. A living, breathing before-and-after shot.

"Can you feel that?" he asked.

She nodded slowly. "Some. Where the grafts are."

"Some of this is a graft?"

"Yes. Not…nothing more than was necessary because I couldn't bear for them to add more scars to my body and…it would never have looked normal anyway. As it is, it's kind of Frankenstein's monster."

"You're hardly a monster," he said.

"Flattery won't get you your way," she said, her tone guarded, hard.

He dropped his hand back to his side. "I don't need flattery. You must see that this is going to be a challenge. We were going to marry, we *wanted* to marry."

"A lifetime ago. A face ago."

"Your face doesn't matter to me."

She laughed, a bitter sound. "For God's sake, Xander, don't lie. It insults us both."

"It doesn't matter. I won't be coy with you, Layna. I have to take a wife someday and when I do it will be because she specifically brings a benefit to my position and to Kyonos as a country. At the moment I think you're the most beneficial wife for me. My personal feelings for you as an individual, or for your looks, have no bearing on anything. I doubt I should be faithful to any woman I marry, so I don't see how wild attraction is an issue, either."

She jerked back as though he'd slapped her. "You're asking me to marry you, knowing you don't truly want me, and admitting to me that you will sleep with other women?"

"I'm being honest with you. It's how I would treat any marriage to any woman."

"And why is it you won't be faithful?"

"Does it matter if you aren't truly vying for the position?"

"Pretend I'm considering it," she said, "indulge my curiosities."

He shrugged, a vague sense of shame washing over him as he looked at the woman he would have promised his life to years ago and spoke of planned faithlessness. As he realized that, had he married her as a beauty queen, he would have been unfaithful to her even then.

He'd been young. In lust, not in love. The center of his own universe. Certain of his absolute entitlement.

The moment he'd gotten hard for another woman he would have had her without a thought, no matter the vows he'd made to Layna, because that was the manner of man he'd been. Now...he had no practice in restraint. In turning away from the various and sundry pleasures of the flesh. He'd spent their years apart bathing in them because if he couldn't get clean, then he would at least cover his transgressions in new layers of sin and hope that people never looked deeper. Hoped that he never had to look deeper.

"I have no practice at being with one woman," he said. "I can't imagine a lifetime with the same person in my bed, and I have low expectations of myself in that regard."

"Especially if your wife is ugly," she said.

"It doesn't matter. It's how things are, it's how I am."

"I thought you were changing."

He shook his head, taking a deep breath. "I came back because it was right, not because I have any burning conviction about the rightness of it. I can't condemn Stavros and Eva to a life they don't want when I was the one who was raised for it from the cradle. And it's one thing to walk away and ignore responsibilities when actually having to rule the country is years in the future. But with the way things are now…with the way Stavros's marriage turned out and the fact that the heir will be up to Eva without me. The fact that my father could die at any moment and a decision had to be made, that changed things. But it didn't change me. The one thing I can give for sure is honesty, so I'm giving that. Or would you rather have lies?"

"I rather wish I would have known you, really known you, back when we were engaged. I don't think I would have been so eager to say yes."

"Back then you had other options, too, but now you only have two—the convent, or standing at my side, ruling a country."

Black fire lit up in her eyes, the kind of anger he'd never seen on her face before, not in the time since he'd walked back into her life, and not in the life before. "You're so quick to remind me of how low I've fallen, but let me take a moment to show you a mirror. Your face might be as beautiful as it ever was, Xander, but you are nothing more than a dead limb on the Drakos family tree. Stavros made something with this country after you destroyed it, Evangelina was brave enough to fight for something she wanted, she didn't just run away. And what have you done?"

"Nothing," he said, his voice rough, his heart beating, bloody and ragged. "I have done nothing, and I would seek to change that. I am *trying* to change that. I made mistakes, Layna, and I will not deny it. I was a hurt, frightened child when I left, and then I became jaded. Now I have no heart left to wound and about a thousand things to atone for. So I am here, and I am trying. I am offering you this, the chance to rule with me. To make a difference. To give you children. Or you can go back to your convent and hide—because you're too afraid to face criticism—and make a small ripple in a giant pond with your good deeds when you could be changing the world. You can accuse me of anything you like, and you're probably right. But if you turn me down, you're turning down a chance to make a real difference."

She snorted, her lip curled. "You say that like marrying you, sharing your bed, is an incidental I shouldn't have to worry my head about so long as I can do my duty."

"Lie back and think of Kyonos," he bit out. He didn't know why he was pushing this so hard. He should let her go. He shouldn't be standing in the hall of his palace all but begging her to marry him. And yet he was.

Because he'd decided that Layna Xenakos would be his wife and now he couldn't fathom it being anyone else. No one would make a better queen. No one would help his image, or his country, in a deeper way than she would.

And he wanted her. That was the end of the reasoning really. When he wanted something, he got it.

"You're disgusting."

"And yet you're still here." He put one hand on the wall behind her and leaned in. "Would it be so bad?"

"You realize that I was prepared to swear off sex for life, that if I take my vows it means no men ever. Do you honestly think you're going to entice me with your looks?"

"Your altruism, then. And the chance to rise above where you fell. The chance to show all of Kyonos that, in the end, you have triumphed. Or, keep hiding."

Layna struggled to catch her breath. Rage, sadness and a deep, dark need all pulled at her. Xander, near enough to touch, smelling like rain and sin and man, was enough to make her pulse go into hyperdrive.

She lied when she said sex wasn't the way to tempt her. She was a woman who was prepared to take vows in part because she believed no man would ever want her, and, he was right, because it was easier to hide than to be out in the world experiencing rejection.

She liked men. And had things not changed the way they had, she never would have chosen a life that meant no men. No marriage. No children.

Children. A chance to make a difference.

She looked at Xander, at his strikingly handsome features. He was as perfect as he'd ever been, and the idea of him stuck with her...it was laughable.

And why are you like this? Because of him. Because he left. Because he left the country to rot in its own hell. And he never once thought of you. You needed him and he was gone.

Yes. It had been his decision to leave. To steal the future she'd always dreamed of for herself. Why couldn't she have it back? But if she was going to take him, the decisions wouldn't be his alone. Not again. He'd had enough control for too long.

He would sacrifice, too. She would not be a martyr. She would have something for herself. And why not? Why ache for a man's touch when she could have it? Why long for the glitter of the palace in deep, secret parts of herself when it could be hers? Why wish that she could have a baby when it could be her reality?

"You can have me," she said, her voice hard, "on one condition."

"What is that?"

"I am the only woman you'll ever have in your bed again."

"I told you already…"

"Yes, and I already told you I wouldn't marry you, but that didn't stop you from building your case and asking again. You don't get to name all the terms, Xander. I am giving up my future at the convent and as much as you belittle it, I did find something there. Peace. With myself. With God and with those around me. You're asking me to leave that, and I'm consenting. To put myself out there before the world and expose myself to ridicule. And I won't do it for free. I won't make all the concessions. From this moment on, you will have no other woman. And you won't have me until vows are made. As I know well given the current state of my life, nothing is final until vows are spoken."

"And if I am unfaithful? If I agree now, but transgress later?"

"I will shame you in the media, your children will know you for the faithless man you are and I will ensure I sign a document that means I get your worldly assets. That's expensive sex, Xander, she would have to be well worth it."

A slow smile curved his lips. "You are quite ruthless under those plain clothes, aren't you?"

"Life has a way of making us that way, doesn't it?"

"I suppose it does."

"You've managed to live through all of this with very little in the way of consequences. Well, consider me your punishment." She turned and walked away from him, shaking with rage and sadness, with the tears that were building inside of her, a hard knot of pressure in her chest that she could hardly breathe past.

She'd just agreed to marry Xander Drakos, to become queen of Kyonos. To share the bed of a man who didn't truly want to be with her. She would never be able to go back to the convent. To the women she considered her friends. Her family.

But she was resolved. She'd made the right decision.

She was taking back a piece of the life that she lost. The life she should have had. It wouldn't be everything, not for either of them. But if felt like her right. She would be queen. A goal she'd fixed herself on at sixteen, from the first moment she'd seen Xander in person at a ball. She would bear the heirs to the throne, children for her to love. The children she'd given up hope of having.

And she would force Xander to face the consequences of his actions, every morning when he woke, and every night when he went to bed.

And she would try to ignore the crawling humiliation that thought made her feel. Tried and failed. As she walked into her bedroom and closed the door, she dissolved into misery, and gave in to her tears.

"I won't be coming back," she said into the phone. It had been hours since she'd accepted Xander's proposal. And now she'd realized she had to call Mother Maria-Francesca and confess.

"I thought you might not."

"You did?"

"He's the reason you were running all this time," she said, her tone calm, steady. "And he's the reason I never advised you to move ahead with your vows.

"He is?"

"You are dedicated, and I have never doubted your faith, so please don't take me wrong, but I always felt you were driven by your inner demons, and not your convictions. It was good that you had us, to give you the shelter that you needed. But this is a calling that requires your whole life. And it requires a drive that goes beyond fear of the world outside."

She nodded slowly. "I know."

Deep down, Layna had always known it was true. Because she had ached for other things. She used convent life to hide from her desires, desires she felt could never be met. So that she didn't have to see gorgeous men, and mothers with babies, clothes there was no point in her wearing, hairstyles that would make no difference because she would never be pretty again.

She was having some of what she wanted. She felt…in some ways she felt more in control than she had in years. This wasn't about Xander, or his hold on her. It was about claiming the life she desired.

But if she had known this was what she really wanted, she never would have imposed on the Sisters.

"I didn't mean to use anyone," she said, her voice choked.

"You gave back more than you ever took, Magdalena."

Layna smiled at the use of the name. "Thank you. I'm not sure that's true, but thank you. I hope…to continue on giving in my new position

I…I suppose I'm going to be a princess. And queen one day."

"I'm glad to hear it."

"I won't forget what you taught me. I'm going to use this. I'm going to do good with my position." Something she wouldn't have cared about if she'd married Xander as a girl of eighteen. She would have just used it to increase her shopping budget.

"That's nice to hear. But you're allowed to want things. You're allowed to have dreams."

"I've tried hard not to have them," she said, wiping away a tear she hadn't realized had escaped.

"I know you have, Layna. You've tried very hard to keep yourself safe. But if I could give you one last piece of advice, it would be not to let fear decide things for you."

"I won't."

And she wouldn't. Her decision was made, and even though the enormity of it made her tremble, there was no going back now.

CHAPTER SEVEN

"I TRUST YOU slept well."

"Your trust is misplaced."

Xander laughed as Layna made her way into the dining room and sat down at the table. He hadn't seen her since she'd run dramatically from him in the hall last night, but he'd had a feeling hunger would ferret her out of her room eventually. And here she was, in time for brunch.

"That is too bad. You haven't changed your mind, have you?"

Hard eyes met his. "No. Sorry, if you were looking for a reprieve you aren't going to get one from me."

"I don't want one."

"Even though you won't be permitted to slake your lusts elsewhere?"

"I've slaked them pretty well over the past fifteen years. More variety than most, so I can't truly complain." Though the idea of monogamy was foreign. Even so, if he promised her fidelity, he would give it. He would hardly sneak around behind her back all for the sake of sex, when he could have it with her if he wanted.

Not for the first time, he was feeling curious about the body beneath those simple shifts. Quite simply, in terms of her looks, he'd been shocked at first. And every time he looked at her, he was shocked. How she'd changed. The extent of the damage. But it was getting easier to let go of. Easier to just accept that it was part of her now.

And honestly, it made him extra curious about her body and if that made him reprehensible, so be it. She was to be his wife, and he hadn't reconciled the scars yet. They didn't turn him off but he wasn't exactly overcome by attraction.

As if to goad his thoughts his gut kicked as she moved into the room, the sunlight spilling over the smooth side of her face, catching fire behind her hair and revealing a golden halo. He got a glimpse of that blonde he'd been missing, subdued without the aid of dye, but there was some there. There was something about her that pulled him to her, there was no mistaking that.

"You will have to be tested," she said, her tone

dry as she took a seat at the table. "I'm not risking catching an STD from you, so I'm sorry if you find that a problem, but you've been around."

"I get tested every six months. I'm promiscuous, but I'm responsibly promiscuous."

"Oxymoron."

"Judge not," he said, looking back down at his food.

"You can judge me all you want in that area of my life. I find myself quite blameless."

He raised a brow and looked back up at her. And found himself unbearably curious. How long had it been since she'd been with a man? Since before the convent? Before the accident?

Had she ever?

A ridiculous thought. She was thirty-three. A woman would have had to have been living in a convent to be a virgin at her age. But then, she had been, so all bets were off.

He found himself unreasonably intrigued by the idea. As if there was any doubt of his debauchery. Being fascinated by her innocence confirmed it.

"I find myself lacking in regret," he said. "Which I suppose isn't the same as blameless."

"That would be a seared conscience," she said.

"And I have no desire to hear about your exploits beyond looking at medical records and seeing a negative result on the test."

"You're a savvy little thing for a woman who's spent ten years in a convent."

"I wasn't born in one."

"I suppose not. I propose that we set the wedding for early spring."

"That's very soon. Only a couple of months."

"I know," he said, "but it will create a nice celebratory atmosphere. Also, you've told me I have to remain celibate until our wedding night so I'm not eager to put it off."

Red bloomed in her cheeks, visible even beneath her scars. "I shouldn't have thought you would be overly concerned with that."

"You thought wrong. Now—" he reached in front of him and pulled a black velvet drape from over a tray that contained six rings, all a part of the Drakos family collection "—I have a selection of rings for you to choose from. There is, of course, the one that you had back when we were engaged the first time. It's sized to fit you, assuming that's stayed the same. But I know that women often change their tastes, so I wanted to give you options."

Layna swallowed hard and stared at the jewelry in front of her. She'd come down hoping for some coffee and fruit. Maybe eggs and bacon. She hadn't expected diamonds. It was, in her opinion, a little early in the morning for diamonds.

She couldn't tear her eyes from the pear-shaped diamond, surrounded by citrines, glittering in the midmorning light that was filtering through the window.

It had been hers. She could still remember King Stephanos asking for it. He'd called her in with her father, deeply regretful to have to ask for it back. But it had also belonged to his wife, and since Xander was now gone and the wedding wouldn't be taking place, he simply couldn't bear to have it out of the palace.

Leaving, her hand had felt bare and her heart…

How could he leave her? How could he leave all of them? And why had she never kissed his lips?

Looking at the ring made her remember all of that. She hated those memories. They made her feel too much. They interrupted her contentment.

But then, her contentment had been interrupted for a while now. Also Xander's fault.

She reached out, her fingers hovering over that ring. It was the one she wanted. She'd been allowed to choose back then, too, and it had been her favorite. But this wasn't the same moment. She wasn't the same girl. He was not the same man.

"I don't care," she said, putting her hand back at her side. "You can choose it for me."

He arched a brow and picked up a ring with a square cut solitaire and an ornate white gold band. "This one, then," he said. "If you don't care."

"I don't."

He stood from his place at the table and walked to where she sat, standing in front of her and taking her hand in his. Then, with her sitting and him looming above her, he slipped the ring onto her finger. "It fits fine, doesn't it?"

She pulled her hand back and curled her fingers into a fist. "Fine," she said, trying to swallow and failing, her throat too dry to manage it.

She looked down at her hand, at the completely different ring that was now on her finger. This was different. This wasn't just going back in time. Recapturing what might have been. He might have the same name, but he was a different man. Just as she was a different woman.

Time had changed them. Time had changed their circumstances. She was no longer half in love with him, that was for sure.

Neither would she be falling in love with him any time soon.

"I do need to go and see my father sometime soon."

She nodded slowly. "I imagine you do."

"And we shall have to plan a party. To celebrate my return, and to celebrate our engagement. And hope it isn't perceived as tacky since my father is ill."

"Maybe you can talk to Stavros about that?"

"Oh, yes, I could talk to Stavros, though it seems he would rather not talk to me."

"Eva, then?"

"I should talk to both of them."

She frowned. "I'm sure we can find a way to make sure it doesn't look tacky. If we try and portray it as a show of strength for the country. No matter how dark the night, the dawn is coming, and so on."

"See," he said, smiling, "this is why I need you."

Those words did something to her. Made her heart feel like it was unfolding, like it was expanding. Made her feel a little bit of pain, a little bit of pleasure. But it was stupid. It wasn't flattering. He only needed her because he was a gigantic PR nightmare. Such a gigantic PR nightmare that a scarred almost-nun looked good by comparison.

"Well, I'll do what I can to help. Though, it's not for you."

"I'm sure it's not."

"It's for my country."

"Do you owe this country anything?" he asked. "After the way they treated you, do you really owe them anything?"

"One man with a cup of acid isn't Kyonos, Xander."

"And one man with a cup of acid shouldn't be your whole life, Layna," he said, his voice rough, his eyes suddenly serious.

"To what do I owe the sincerity?"

"I don't like seeing you hurt."

"Then why are you so often the one who hurts me?" she asked, her newly unfurled heart closing tightly again. Like a flower suddenly deprived of sunlight.

"It's a gift I have," he said, looking away from her, out the window. "It's what I seem to do. I hurt people who genuinely don't deserve it." He looked back at her. "I guess that's your warning. You can back out now if you want."

Something in his eyes sent a shock through her. It was a window into his pain. It hadn't been there fifteen years ago, but it was there now, as obvious as if he'd spoken about it out loud. In that brief moment she had the sense that she was standing on the edge of a chasm, looking down into an abyss that had no end.

It frightened her. And it made him impossible to turn away from.

"You couldn't possibly hurt me any more than I've already been hurt." Even as she said it, she had a feeling it was a lie. She hadn't kissed him yet, much less gone to bed with him. She hadn't heard about the wounds he carried deep inside of himself.

He knew it was a lie, too. She could tell by the way his lips curved up, could tell now, that the expression was false. That there was no real humor in it. No real warmth. "Well then, we had better make a formal announcement."

"I suppose we'd better."

"You will need a dress, for the engagement party. I trust you won't mind if I use a professional shopper to select one for you?"

She blinked. "No."

"Then I shall have your measurements done and that will be taken care of as quickly as possible."

"What about your father?" she asked.

"I should go and visit him alone."

Except she had a feeling that he shouldn't. She wasn't sure why. And moreover, she wasn't sure why she should care. Why his pain should interest her or concern her in any way, and yet over the course of the past few seconds she found that it did.

"I'll go with you. It will help solidify your plans. When you announce your engagement… I think your father felt very bad about what happened to me," she said.

"He did?"

"He was consumed by his own grief."

"Yes," Xander said, "I know."

"But he came to see me once. I…I didn't want

to talk to him so I pretended to be asleep, but I knew he came."

"Why didn't you want to talk to him?"

"I was just starting to realize, really realize, that nothing in my life was ever going to be the same. That my face wasn't going back to normal. That... that I had maybe twenty surgeries ahead of me."

"Twenty?" he asked.

"It ended up being twenty-one. Skin grafts and reconstruction. Some of the grafts didn't take and...anyway. I knew that I had all kinds of hell ahead and that everything I knew was behind me. I didn't...it was hard to face people. That way you looked at me at the convent, when you realized it was me...it was ten times worse than that every time someone saw me right after the attack happened. I looked like something from a bad zombie movie. And the press said that. More than once. I hardly looked real at all. And it made my mother cry. It made my father sick. I got tired of seeing the expressions so I would close my eyes when visitors would come. And then it was just easier to keep them that way."

"Then of course you can come," he said, his tone light, as though he was content to skip over the graveness of the subject matter. And that suited her just fine. Being with him had forced her to relive her past more than she was comfortable with. "I'm sure my father will be happy to see you."

"I'm sure he'll be overjoyed to see you."

That smile again. That fake smile. "I wouldn't bet on it. But it will be nice to have you there to take some of the focus off of me."

Xander kept finding reasons to put off visiting his father, although, Layna was hardly going to judge him for avoidance since she was a pro at it.

Not that she could blame him. She imagined he was hardly going to have the fatted calf slaughtered in his oldest son's honor when he learned of Xander's return.

The engagement had been announced. On that he hadn't procrastinated. And the date of the ball had been set.

In spite of the fact that he was being hammered by the press, he was soldiering forward.

Prince Stavros and his wife, Jessica, and Princess Eva and her husband, Mak, were set to attend. Which would make for an interesting evening, Layna was sure. She imagined that things wouldn't be easy between Xander and his brother.

She tried to breathe around the terror that started constricting her throat when she thought about exposing herself to all of those people. All of that scrutiny. And Xander had said a selection of dresses would be here soon.

As if cued by her thoughts, there was a knock at the door. But rather than the woman who had come in to take her measurements earlier in the day, she was greeted by Xander, who had a black garment bag in his hand.

"Where's Patrice?" she asked.

"Downstairs having a coffee. I told her this would be between me and my fiancée." He stepped into the room and closed the door behind him and her heart collided with her breastbone.

"It doesn't sound like she's busy. Perhaps you'd like to trade places with her."

"No," he said.

"You work too hard," she said, no conviction in her voice.

"Now, *agape mou*, you and I both know that's not true." He sat down on her bed, the grin on his face wicked, and she felt her entire body tighten like a spool of wire.

That endearment. He'd called her that during their first engagement, too. *My love.* He hadn't meant it then and she was sure he didn't mean it now.

"So what…I'm supposed to put on a fashion show for you?"

"If you wish."

"Some might call it a freak show."

He stood quickly, the motion fluid, shocking. "Let us get one thing straight here and now," he said. "I will not stand for the press speaking of you in any terms that are not flattering. I will not hear it from you, either."

"Why should you care?" she asked. "It's true enough. I'm more sideshow than beauty pageant and we both know that."

"I damn well do not," he growled, advancing on her. "Is that truly what you think?"

"Can you tell me I'm beautiful?"

The fire in his eyes cooled. "No," he said, his voice hushed now, an extinguished flame. "Can you tell me I'm good?"

"No." She ached now. His denial like salt on a

wound, but then, what would it have mattered if he would have said yes? It wouldn't have. It would have been a lie all the same and they both would have known it.

"You are, though," he said. "Good, that is. And isn't that the better thing to be?"

"When a camera is pointed at me I think I would prefer the beauty."

"When trials come, it would be better to be you, trust me. Now—" he handed her the garment bag "—it is time for us to preview your dress."

She held the bag to her chest and walked into the bathroom. She wasn't beautiful, but she was good. Wasn't the sort of woman to drive a man to passion, but she was good. She turned that over in her mind as she put on the dress, too distracted, too numb to pay much attention to it.

The trouble was, with Xander, she didn't feel particularly good. He made her feel edgy. Angry. Hot and unpredictable. With him around she did things like accept marriage proposals and demand he sleep only with her.

Which meant he would be sleeping with her.

Her hands shook as she did up the zipper at the back of the dress. She'd sort of bet on dying a virgin. She wasn't thrilled with it, really, but she hadn't seen another way.

The idea of being with him… She wanted him. No point in denying it. She just wished she was certain he wanted her.

She opened the bathroom door and stepped out into the bedroom. She caught sight of herself in the reflection of the mirror just behind the bed, behind Xander, and froze for a moment. The dress was…well, it was much more revealing than anything she'd worn in ages. And more sophisticated than the saucy dresses she'd chosen as a teenage girl.

It was black, with a neckline that plunged down to the middle of her chest. "I would need duct tape," she said, looking at her breasts, which were attempting to make an escape. The chiffon fabric skimmed her curves and fell to the floor in a ripple, flowing as she moved. It was nearly demure, understated. If not for that neckline.

She looked to Xander and realized that his focus was also on her breasts, not that she should be terribly surprised. Because he *was* a man. Still, she was surprised because he was a man who was looking at her. And she was even more surprised because far from being offended, it made her feel warm and a little bit excited.

"What do you think?" she asked.

"I like it," he said, his voice rough.

"It's…not anything like what I would normally wear."

"No, and that's a good thing. You aren't wearing one of those flowered monstrosities to our engagement party."

"But…people will look at me."

"Yes," he said, his voice rough. "I imagine they will."

"I don't want them to look at me," she said.

"But they will, *agape*. You're to be the princess, one day their queen. You were a woman they all cared about, a woman they adored, back when you were first engaged to be married to me. Their eyes will be on you no matter what you wear. Better that when they look they see a woman with confidence."

"But I don't think I have any," she said.

He moved to her. "You should."

"Why?"

"Because you are the woman most deserving

of the crown. You should hold your head high if only for that reason."

He lifted his hand and reached behind her, taking hold of the pins in her hair and releasing the hair from its bun, letting it fall around her face in soft waves. He had touched her hair before, and it had been an oddly sensual experience. His touch, combined with the intense expression on his face, was taking things somewhere beyond sensual now.

He was making her knees kind of weak. Making it hard to breathe.

But he didn't even think she was beautiful.

"We should practice," he said.

"Practice what?"

"They'll expect us to dance."

"Will they?"

"Yes. See? All eyes on us, no matter what you wear. And we need to put up a good front. Because salacious details about my past keep ending up on the front page."

"What now?" she asked.

"'How Many Lovers for the Dishonorable Heir?'"

"Oh, my."

"Yes, indeed."

"And...how many?" she asked.

"Not answering. And I don't know."

"Oh."

"Yes, well. I'm not exactly proud of my behavior. But I am good at dancing."

"This is all so... Oh." He wrapped his arm around her waist and pulled her against his body. Then he took her hand in his, rough and hot, not an aristocrat's hands. But then, he hadn't been living an aristocrat's life.

"Do you know how to dance still, or is that forbidden for a novice?" he asked, leading her into the first step of a slow dance to no music.

"I'm out of practice," she said, trying hard not to lose her breath. He was so warm and hard, and she was pressed up against him.

And in that moment she realized just how very much she wanted him. A deep, burning ache that spread from her core and ignited in the rest of her body. Such a strange thing. Lust was one of the little luxuries that had to be put away for the kind of life she'd been trying to lead, but she was all but bathing in it now.

She was so aware of his hand on her waist, his

fingers entwined with hers. With each breath he took and how it made his chest rise to meet her breasts, how it made her nipples feel tight. Made her feel desperate for more. More of his touch. More of him.

"So am I," he said.

"You don't seem like it."

"Well, there isn't much in the way of formal ballroom dancing in the casinos I frequent."

"Is that all you've done since you left?"

"Basically. I live in the casinos, literally. I don't own a home. There's never been any point."

"You make money gambling?"

He lifted a shoulder and kept dancing. "I have a gift."

"You're a card counter, aren't you?"

"Not on purpose. But if I happen to be a bit more observant than the average person, is it my fault?"

"You really are a bad man."

He chuckled, slow and deep, the sound rumbling through him, and her, sending shock waves of sensation through her body. "And I don't even work at it. It just comes naturally. How about you?" he asked.

"How about me what?"

"Do you have to work at being good?"

She blinked. "Um…I don't know really. In some ways, no. But then, what I do…I don't do it because it's good. I do it because I don't have anything else to do. Because…maybe because it's easy to be good if you don't want much of anything. I could never have gone to hide out at a casino, for example, because I had no desire to be around anyone. I couldn't go sleep my way through Europe like you because I didn't want anyone to see me, much less sleep with me. And I could hardly go get drunk because you aren't supposed to mix alcohol and pain pills," she said, dryly. "All things considered, I don't know that I get any brownie points for good behavior."

"You haven't seemed particularly saintly since I've seen you, I'll tell you that in all honesty." His fingers moved down on her waist, just an inch or so, but enough to edge into somewhat erotic territory. At least, erotic for a woman who hadn't had a kiss in…ever, and was due. Past due.

"Maybe it's because I…I feel like I'm waking up." It was the strangest thing, but as she spoke the words she knew that was the best way to describe it. It was like she'd been sleeping. All those years after the attack, and then at the convent, it had been like hovering between reality and a dream. There was a cushion there, between her and life, and she had needed it.

Now, though, her eyes were wide open, and everything was clear. Frightening. And amazing.

"I thought women needed to be kissed awake," he said, lowering his head, his mouth a whisper away from hers.

"Sleeping Beauty maybe," she said. "But we both know that I'm not—"

He silenced her with the firm pressure of his lips on hers. She was almost too shocked to register the feeling of the kiss. She felt it deeper than she'd imagined she would. Felt it in the pit of her stomach just as strongly as she felt it against her lips.

It was brief, and it was very nearly chaste, but it tilted her world on its axis completely. And he had no idea, she was sure of that. Because for him, it was just another kiss. But for her it was the first.

"How was that?" he asked.

"I…" She pulled away from him. "I don't think that had anything to do with dancing."

"It had to do with us, as a couple, making our

debut at the engagement party, where we'll be dancing. It was a natural extension."

Yes, a natural extension for him, but not for her.

"Well, there's no need for any of that until after…until…"

"You aren't part of a convent anymore," he said, "you're a woman."

"I've been a woman the entire time, thank you. It didn't change when I went to the convent, it didn't change when I left. It didn't change just because you decided to kiss me. Our marriage is based on necessity, not on passion, so let's not pretend."

"Who said I was pretending?"

"Right, Xander, I'm sure you were overwhelmed by lust when you told me that I wasn't beautiful only twenty minutes ago."

"There is something else," he said, his voice tight, strange. "Something…"

She shook her head. "Just don't lie to me."

"This," he said, looking down, "it doesn't lie. I would put your hand on me but I think that would be a step too far."

"Put my hand on…" Her stomach tightened

painfully and she looked down, her eyes following the line his gaze had. "Oh."

"I thought it might be off-limits."

"Yes," she said, her throat dry. "It is. Definitely in the post-marriage vow zone. Anything below the belt."

"You look much more intrigued than you do offended."

"Do I? That's just the shock talking. Well, not talking, forming my facial expressions for me. I'm terribly shocked."

"I look forward to shocking you a bit more after our marriage vows then."

"Don't make it a joke, please," she said, suddenly feeling like she needed to lie down. Or dissolve into a gigantic puddle of wimpy girl tears. "I know you're experienced and cavalier and having pity sex with an ugly girl is just a witty anecdote waiting to happen for you. But this isn't funny to me. It's my life. And I'm the one who stands to be hurt the most by this. I'm the one…"

"You're the one who called yourself my punishment, Layna. I have said nothing cruel to you on that score. I don't look at you and think that you're ugly—neither do I feel like I'm doing you any great favors by marrying you and sharing your bed. In truth, you may find that you are more unhappy with the demanded fidelity than I am."

"Why is that?"

"Because it will ensure that I'm around more, and you may tire of me quickly. You have this idea that I'm somehow more desirable stock because I'm not scarred. Let me assure you that while I may be physically undamaged, you are not by any stretch getting the better end of this deal. I am selfish, I have spent the majority of the past few years battling demons and addictions, and doing neither very well at all. You may think that what I'm giving you is pity sex, but don't for one moment think that I don't realize what I have on my hands is a pity marriage."

She blinked back tears, his words settling over her like a heavy cloak, making it hard to breathe. "I don't pity you. I don't approve of you. I'm not sure that I like you, but I don't pity you. This is…a marriage of no one's convenience. What we do, we do for our country. And…I do it for children. Because I do want them. And I had thought that wasn't possible for me, so to have the chance…I do want it. Power is something I don't crave anymore, status is almost my enemy because it means I'll be under scrutiny."

"A marriage born of a sense of national duty and disdain then," he said, dryly. "You flatter me."

"I would imagine you've been flattered enough in your life that you don't require much from me."

"I'm sure my ego can weather it."

"I'm not sure mine will survive any of this."

"It will," he said, his tone certain, authoritative. And in that moment, she saw a hint of the king he would be. So strange, because she knew the boy he'd been. Cocky and obnoxious in so many ways, but handsome as sin and just as tempting. She'd barely gotten to know the man he was now, wounded, damaged and self-deprecating. As much as the boy had loved himself, she had a feeling the man hated himself just as much.

But for one second, all of that fell away. And she saw nothing more than confidence. Nothing more than a smooth, unswerving focus.

"This is why I'm marrying you," she said, her voice hushed now. "Because I believe that, no matter where you've been in the past, your future is tied to Kyonos. That with you we will rise or fall, and if we fall it will be because the people can't get past what has been done. You leaving…"

"Me killing the queen," he said.

"You didn't kill her," she said. "You were driving, but it was an accident. It was…"

"People think it, Layna. Just as the man who threw acid on you, trying to get to your father blamed him for his troubles."

"Then this is why," she said, suddenly feeling the need to close the gap between them. To make contact. "This is why I'm marrying you. Because if I can help in any way, if I can heal some of the wounds from that time, I will do it. Because you are the future here, Xander."

He frowned and lifted his other hand, touched her damaged cheek with his thumb. "It is a shame that time won't heal your wounds."

"It is."

"Sometimes I think it won't heal mine, either." He released his hold on her and turned and walked out of her room, leaving her standing there in an evening gown, in the middle of the day, more confused than she'd ever been in her life.

CHAPTER EIGHT

HELL. XANDER HAD forgotten how much he hated these kinds of events.

The engagement celebration was small compared to some of the parties thrown at the Kyonosian palace, due to the short notice and out of respect for the king's health.

Xander's recently noisy conscience pricked him. He should go and see the king. It was a hard thing to do. The last time he'd stood before the old man, his father said in no uncertain terms that he blamed Xander for the queen's death.

And because he hadn't been wrong, Xander had finally done what Stavros, and the man who believed he was Xander's father, had wanted. He left.

Because it had been easier for everyone. And it had been easy, most especially, for him.

He wasn't truly the heir after all.

You can't tell him, Xander. You have to be king.

You are my firstborn son and the right should be yours, regardless of the mistakes I've made.

Xander shut out the sound of his mother's pleading voice. He hated reliving that conversation. Mainly because it was the last one they'd ever had. It had changed everything.

He straightened and looked across the room at Layna. She looked…well, she did look beautiful in her way.

She was wearing makeup. He'd brought in a team to help her get ready. He wondered if she'd ever bothered to put makeup on her face, or if it had been too discouraging. There was no hiding the fact that the skin was damaged on one side. It looked…aged with makeup on, rather than just scarred.

But her eyes were highlighted to perfection, and they glowed with golden warmth, her lips painted a deep rose. And that dress. That dress that made his body tighten. That made him want…

He wanted her, and that was the most surprising thing about this arrangement. He hadn't expected to want her. He'd had an endless array of models, mainstream actresses and actresses who did the kinds of movies that rarely had scenes outside the bedroom. Women who were perfectly beautiful, either by birth or with the aid of a surgeon's knife.

He'd hardly thought Layna would present a temptation to him, all things considered.

And yet...when he'd kissed her the other day, she had been a surprise. A burst of flavor on his lips unlike any he'd ever tasted before. And newness, to a man as jaded as himself, was so unexpected it was an aphrodisiac that was almost unmatched.

"Congratulations are in order, I suppose."

Xander turned to face Stavros, and Eva, who was standing next to him, a glowing smile on her face, her hand over her rounded belly. He wanted to embrace them both. But he didn't know if he could. And that was a strange thing.

Who didn't feel they could hug their siblings if they wanted to? Who didn't speak to their siblings for fifteen years?

Eva had gone from a child to a woman in that time. Having a child of her own. Stavros was a man as well, not the teenage boy he'd been.

Theos. He felt old.

And more than a little bit tired.

"For both of you as well," he said, keeping back, his hands clasped behind him.

"I'm surprised she agreed to marry you," Stavros said, his eyes flashing over to Layna, who seemed to be shrinking into the corner under the watchful eyes of their many guests.

"Are you?" he asked. "We had an agreement before I left."

"And things have changed."

"I've noticed," he said.

Eva smiled, shy but with a glimmer of that old sparkle in her eyes. "Xander, I'm glad you're back. I don't want things to be weird between us. So let's skip all of the regret and angry stuff. I'll leave that to you and Stavros, since I doubt he'll let it go as fast as I will. I, for one, have missed you for too long, and I won't waste a second of you being back here with anger."

"I appreciate that, Eva," he said, feeling strangely tight around the chest. "I plan on staying."

Stavros frowned. "I would love to never speak to you again. But you're going to be the king. And my wife tells me that I should be nice because not only are you the future king, you are the uncle to our children, and it would be wrong of me to deprive you or them of that relationship."

"She threatened you, didn't she?" Eva asked, smiling.

"I don't want to sleep on the couch for the rest of my life," Stavros said, his tone dry. "But someday…we'll have to talk more. And someday, perhaps I will not be so angry. But not today."

Xander nodded. "Yes." But he knew they wouldn't talk about everything. Never about everything.

He made the rounds with Stavros and Eva, meeting Stavros's wife, Jessica, and their two children, and Eva's husband, Mak.

He looked back at Layna, who was slinking into the wall now, fading. "Excuse me," he said, "I have to go and ask a woman to dance."

He didn't want to see her do this. Didn't want to watch her try and disappear, and he wasn't even certain why. Why it should matter.

It shouldn't. She would get him the positive press he needed, she was a worthy choice to produce heirs. Nothing beyond that should matter.

But it did.

"Are you trying to turn into another coat of paint?" he asked, when he was near to her.

"What?"

"You look like you're trying to become part of the wall," he said.

"You left me alone and I feel...I feel self-conscious."

"You look..."

She shook her head. "Don't."

"But you do."

"Compared to the way I usually look."

"So I'm not allowed to win?"

She blinked, dark lashes fanning over high cheekbones. "Thank you."

"Of course. Now, you will come and dance with me and stop acting like you wish you could melt into the floor."

She looked stricken. "We're really going to dance?"

"That's why we practiced, darling." He extended his hand and she looked at him like he was offering her forbidden fruit. He felt like he was. Like he was on the verge of bringing her into something he had no right to drag her in to.

But it was too late. She was here. In front of

hundreds of people, his ring glittering on her finger, tomorrow's headlines being created right now, in the moment.

He didn't deserve to use her like this. To have her as a buffer between himself and the unflattering headlines about his past behavior. But he didn't see another choice.

Delicate fingers wrapped around his and she allowed him to lead her to the dance floor. He pulled her to him, much more gently than he'd done in her room.

"Relax," he said, his lips near her ear.

He breathed in deep, and her scent teased him. It wasn't false, or floral. It was the wind. The sea. The grass. Skin. It was Kyonos. It made his stomach tighten, opened up a well of longing, a strange sense of need and homesickness that washed over him like a wave.

This desire for her came from somewhere deep. It didn't come from looking at her, or even from touching her, it was her very presence. It seemed to be some part of her, some part deep inside, connecting with something in him.

Perhaps it was shared pain meeting a shared goal. Or maybe it was nothing more complex than a bout of celibacy that had gone on for too many months. Either way, it was beginning to feel too strong to fight. He was wondering if there was a reason to bother, anyway.

She was going to be his wife after all.

Not that she had any idea of what that truly meant. Of who he truly was.

"Everyone is staring, aren't they?" she asked.

"Have you ever worn makeup? Since your attack?"

She frowned. "Once. I tried it once. Not very long after my last surgery. It didn't really help I… But I thought tonight I should wear some because I needed to dress up and…"

"You look lovely. And I do mean that."

"They did a better job covering the damage than I ever managed to do."

"That isn't the only reason."

"Let's not do this mushy, stumbling lying thing now, Xander. You were perfectly honest with me the other day about my looks. So don't go trying to smooth it all over just because I tried."

"You are a stubborn woman," he said. "And I want you."

"I don't understand."

"You don't understand want? Desire? Do you know what it means to want someone?"

"I…yes. But I don't need you to lie to me about it."

"I'm not." he said, tightening his hold on her, bringing her curves flush against his body. And he let her feel what she was doing to him. He let his cock harden against her and he didn't bother to suppress his need, his fantasies. He imagined what it would be like to have her bare softness against him, without this damned tux in the way.

What it would be like to make her let go. To make her break out of the little cell she'd locked herself in. The one that meant there was no passion. No desire. Only boring, staid contentment.

He wanted to make her lose herself while he lost himself in her. Because for some reason he felt sure that she was the only one who could make him feel again. The only one who might make a change in him that could last.

The feeling that came with that thought was fleeting, but so intense it nearly buckled his knees. So intense he nearly dragged her from the dance floor and into the nearest dark alcove to make her his without any thought to vows.

But then it cleared. The fire dying down as suddenly as it had flared up.

No, there was no changing him. Not even she could do it. There was no magic to be found on her lips. But there was pleasure. And he was a man who'd spent years consumed by the desire for pleasure.

That was the simple answer to why he felt so drawn to her. It wasn't in his nature to deny himself anything he wanted.

"I'm sorry, I wasn't able to hold myself back this time. You accused me of lying about wanting you and I thought you should know this time, for yourself, that it's true."

She pushed out of his arms and walked away from him, leaving him there in the middle of the dance floor, shocked and hard as hell.

He followed her, through the crowd of people and out onto the balcony. Her shoulders were shaking and guilt stabbed him, low in the gut.

He'd had a lot of bad feelings since returning home. Guilt and regret. He preferred it when his life boiled down to being drunk and horny, but right now he had felt sober, horny and guilty.

Which was a combination he wouldn't wish on anyone.

"What did I do? Did I offend you with my erection? Because you're going to have to get used to it if you honestly want to marry me."

She whirled around to face him. "Oh, please. Stop making this about you when it's clearly about me."

"I think we both think it's all only about us."

"Fine," she said, tears on her cheeks, "but…this is…why do you want me? Why…I don't understand this. Any of it."

"Is that really what upset you?"

"It's just a lot. A lot to take. Everything has changed in the past week. Everything I'm supposed to want."

"Do you want me?"

"Xander…"

He walked over to where she was standing and took her chin between his thumb and forefinger. "Do you want me?"

"That's not what this is about."

"But it's part of marriage."

"So is love. We barely have like."

"I'm not big on love," he said. "Personally, I

would rather have want. So if that's all we have, I'm okay with it."

She shook her head. "I can't deal with this just now. Not when everyone is in there and we're on show. I've probably already ruined things by storming out."

"It's okay. I might have been a little bit inappropriate. But I'm out of practice when it comes to civilized behavior."

"You make me…you do make me want things, Xander. Things that I thought I'd let go of. And it scares me. Because in my experience, wanting things is just a long road paved with pain."

"That's emotion you're thinking of. Sex can be a lot more simple. And a lot more fun."

She laughed, a shaky, watery sound. "Well, I wouldn't know."

His gut tightened, blood rushing to his arousal. "I could show you."

"I don't understand this. I don't remember being this tempted by you back when I thought you were a decent human being, so how can I be so drawn to you now?"

"Lust doesn't have to make sense, Layna."

"I guess not," she said, looking at him with a

weary expression. "Perhaps that's why the church has such a firm stance on it. It could potentially get someone into a lot of trouble. Particularly since our bodies seem to be indiscriminate."

"Is your body being indiscriminate for me?" he asked. So strange how badly he just wanted her to say it. How much he wanted to her to admit, from her prim little mouth, that she wanted him. That she was picturing sweaty, tangled limbs and screams of pleasure.

Yes, screams. He wanted it loud. And he wanted it dirty. He wanted it with a ferocity that shook him to his core.

With a woman who's most likely a virgin. You truly are a rare breed of ass.

Maybe. Did it matter? He was so past the point of redemption anyway. And she was going to be his wife, surely that made it at least partly okay.

And if not, why should he start caring now?

It was too late for him anyway.

"We should go back inside," she said.

"You didn't answer my question."

"And I'm not going to. Here I've stormed out of the ballroom and I'm supposed to be making you look stable. So I think it's time to go back and show solidarity, don't you?"

He nodded slowly. She really was good at this. He'd all but forgotten the ball happening inside. If she'd let him he probably would have just lifted her dress and taken her here on the balcony with the ocean as the backdrop. And people just inside.

He did a much better job of thinking of his own appetites than he did of thinking of his people.

"Can I do it?" he asked, not sure why the words came out just then.

"Can you do what?"

"This," he said. Too late to take them back now.

"Will I really be a good king? For some reason, you seem very confident in me when it comes to that part of things. You have no respect for me on a personal level, but you seem very sure that I'll rule well, why?"

"Because you don't want it," she said. "Because there's nothing easy about it, and the power itself doesn't seem to appeal to you at all. What better man to rule?"

"Because I *don't* want it?"

"Yes. From that I have to assume that your motives are pure."

"My motives are a lot of things. But I doubt they're pure. I doubt anything in me is."

"Are you ready to go back?" she asked.

He was humbled in that moment, by her strength. By the cost of this to her. It was costing him, but what really? His total waste of a life? His meaningless flings with random women? His chance to continue living in different penthouse suites?

It was costing her every shred of pride she had.

He would not let them take it. She was too strong. Standing there with her focus fixed on the ballroom, determined to go back in even though he knew it was difficult for her.

"Yes, *agape*, let's go and show them what the future of their country looks like."

CHAPTER NINE

SHE HONESTLY HAD no idea what her problem was. Why she'd melted down with Xander, why she'd had to run out of the ballroom.

Well, no, she did know why. It was because she had no idea what she was doing. She didn't know how to handle men. Didn't know how to deal with this desire that was starting to wrap itself around her like a creeping vine.

This wasn't supposed to happen.

She was supposed to be…at the very least she was supposed to feel nothing for him. And at most, she'd been willing to allow herself to be angry.

And she was angry. She was angry at him for leaving her. She was angry at life for making her the way that she was.

But in there somewhere, she wanted him, too, and that was the thing she couldn't quite deal with.

She breathed in the sea air. It was such a relief

to be outside. To be on the beach instead of in that ballroom, which, as expansive as it was, had made her feel claustrophobic beyond words.

She'd escaped as soon as she could. Most everyone had gone and she'd made her excuses, as soon as was polite. She was dreading tomorrow's headlines. Dreading the future. So funny, because she hadn't thought of the future at all in a long time.

All of her days had been so alike at the convent. Her future had been so certain. So solid. She'd seen her days stretching out before, a calm and endless sea.

But now she was storm-tossed and she had no idea where she would land.

She sat down, not caring that the ground was wet, not caring that there would be sand on her gorgeous black dress. She would hardly be able to wear it again anyway. That was something she remembered from her socialite days. Never wear the same thousand-euro dress twice. Such a sharp contrast to her other life, where she wore the same threadbare shifts until they couldn't be mended anymore.

She felt like she wasn't wholly the girl she'd been before, or the woman she'd become, but damned if she had any idea who she really was. And she blamed Xander for that feeling.

She'd been fine before he'd walked back into her life. She'd been at peace with her choices. And now he was demanding so much from her. So much more than she ever thought she'd have to give to anyone.

"I thought perhaps I had seen a ghost." She looked up and saw Xander standing there, his shirt open at the collar, his tie and jacket discarded.

"That's how I felt the day I saw you at the convent."

"I'm sure."

"What are you doing down here?"

"I might ask you the same thing."

"I am…brooding. I think that's what this is called."

He sat down next to her. "I'll brood with you."

"Brooding is best done alone."

"Doesn't that get tiring, though?"

"What?" she asked.

"Being alone."

She looked out across the water, at the moon reflecting on the waves. "You're never alone, though, are you? I mean, you've never had to be. You've basically been at a giant party for the past few years."

"I've been surrounded by people, yeah. But it's amazing what a hell that can be."

"I doubt you've spent one night alone when you didn't want to be alone," she said, feeling bitter now. Because all she'd had was an endless void of alone. In that huge house without her family, with only a couple of servants to help her with things. Making sure she ate, making sure she didn't overdose on her pain medication.

Locking up her pain medication. And then, when they'd taken her one bit of solace, they'd felt like her enemies, not her allies. Even though she knew differently now.

Xander truly had no idea how isolating her life had been. How low she'd gone. How dark it had been. Because he'd walked away. Because he hadn't stayed. When things had gotten hard in his life he'd left her there, but there had been no way for her to unzip her damaged skin and crawl out of her own body. There had been no way to escape her pain.

"I'm sure getting smashed in a casino was terrible for you, but while you were doing that, I was by myself in my parents' old home in a prescription drug haze, so excuse me if I don't feel that sorry for your plight."

"Layna..."

"No." She stood up. "I wasn't going to tell you this, and for what? My pride? What pride have I got? No, you should know. You should know because you should have been there, Xander. You should have been there with me. I..." A sob broke through, tears spilling down her cheeks. "I needed you..." The words were torn from her, pulling at any thread of dignity she might have had, but they were the truth. A truth she'd never even allowed herself to think before, let alone voice.

She wiped a tear from her cheek. "Do you have any idea... Sometimes I just wanted to be held and there was no one there. And it should have been you. You were supposed to be my husband, you weren't supposed to leave me."

"I won't leave again," he said, his voice rough. "Though...I don't know that I would have done everything for you that you hoped I might."

"Anything would have been better than being alone. My days just kind of blended and...I got addicted to my pain medication. It was so much nicer to be out of it than it was to feel. And the medicine helped with that. Helped things seem nicer. Without them it was just endless despair and…and I would think things like…if I walked out to the beach and went out into the ocean and just…kept walking until the water went over my head, would anyone care? Would I care? Or would everything just stop hurting?"

He swore. "Layna, I'm sorry."

"Why couldn't you help me? Why couldn't you think of anyone but yourself?"

"Because," he said. "Because I killed my mother, Layna. Because my father looked me in the eye and told me he believed it was my fault, and my brother thought so, too. Because I couldn't stay here and face that. And I might never have thought of walking into the ocean but everything I've done has been about seeing that I shorten my days in a very spectacular fashion."

Her chest felt tight. And for the first time she really thought about him, and his loss. Not just her own need. "Did they really blame you?"

"Yes."

"That's not fair, it was an accident."

He nodded slowly. "But we were arguing. And no one knows that but me. I was angry, and so I wasn't paying attention. I looked up and there was a truck cutting across the line and I swerved and hit the side of the mountain because I panicked and overcorrected. They were my mistakes, and they were brought about largely by my anger. Because I didn't take the time to pull the car over. Because I let emotion take over and I behaved… I was stupid. And it was my fault." He looked at her. "Maybe I should have stayed for you. But I don't think I could have been the man you needed. I know I wasn't the man that you thought I was."

"I've never told anyone before," she said. "I've never told anyone about wanting to…about having trouble living. I don't even like to remember it but…do you know what's nice?"

"What?"

"Even when I told you, even when I let myself think about it, I can remember how bad it was, but it doesn't make me feel the way I did then."

"The convent is what changed things for you?"

"It gave me a purpose. I didn't know what to do with myself. I didn't have you. The marriage wasn't going to happen, I wasn't going to be queen. No other man would marry me. My friends, who I took such delight in cutting down behind their backs, wouldn't see me. No one invited me to parties, and I wouldn't have wanted to go if they had. Everything changed for me and all of that combined with my depression just made me...I was just drifting. But after talking to the Sisters after my last surgery, about the work they did, about the life they led, I thought maybe the answer wasn't trying to go back, or even making myself want to go back, but to find something new."

"That's sort of what I did. Only without the altruism or chastity."

"How so?"

"I changed everything. Because things were too different to be who I'd been before."

"That's sort of how I feel right now," she said, turning to face him. "Too different to be the girl I was fifteen years ago, and not quite the woman I was a week ago when you found me again."

"I am sorry," he said. "I'm sorry I've uprooted your life again. And that you were alone. It's funny," he continued, "you're right, I never spent a night alone unless I wanted to. But it's a strange thing about sex. For a moment, there's this clash of heat. A connection of some kind. Ten minutes of euphoria, and then, in the end, you can be skin-to-skin with someone, inside of them, and feel more alone than you ever have in your life." He stood up, hands in his pockets. "There's nothing more terrifying than that. Because it's moments like those where you realize how far beyond human connection you are."

"Is that how you feel?" she asked, the picture he pained cutting a swath of pain through her heart.

"It's just not in me anymore. To love someone. To feel all that deeply. I care about the country, but what I do…it comes from my head."

"Is that a warning?"

He nodded slowly. "Maybe. I don't want to hurt you, it's clear to me that I've done that enough for one lifetime. But we will make a marriage, a real one. We don't need love for that. And…I will be faithful to you."

"You said that already."

"I did say it, but I'm not sure I meant it. I do now. Because I gave it some thought, and what it comes down to is that I know the kind of pain infidelity causes. Even if one party never finds out, there are always consequences."

"What else is there, Xander?" she asked. Because she could sense, somehow, that there was more he wanted to say. That his pain came from somewhere even deeper.

"There isn't anything."

"Really?"

He shook his head. "It's not important." He cleared his throat. "Tomorrow we're going to go and see my father."

"Both of us," she said, confirming it.

"Yes."

"I was going anyway. For my part, Xander, you're not going to be alone anymore. And neither am I."

CHAPTER TEN

HE COULDN'T HIDE the headlines from her forever. But he would do his best. He had expected… something triumphant. Something about Layna's bravery. About her beauty, at least her inner beauty, to grace the pages of the newspapers. But he was disappointed.

There were before and after photos. Layna, young, radiant and golden, and Layna as she was now. With the scars that had changed the landscape of her face.

And they asked would she now be the face of the nation. And suddenly…suddenly they were acting like he was a saint. Honoring past commitments in spite of present circumstances.

Isn't that what you wanted?

His blood boiled. Rage spiking through him. At the media. At himself. He had used her. He had exposed her to this.

And he would protect her from it as long as

he could. Because he needed her. Of that he was certain. He had no idea how he would rule without her.

He couldn't dwell on it now. Today he was seeing his father. Today, he was facing the hardest part of his past.

At least Layna would be beside him.

His father was an old man. That was his first thought when he walked into the hospital room and saw the man he'd always thought of as so imposing, hooked up to all the machinery.

He was asleep. Or maybe he was unconscious. Xander wasn't sure. He wasn't certain he could get close enough to find out.

Delicate fingers wrapped around his hand and he looked down at the top of Layna's head. Shocked that she was there. Shocked that she was touching him.

"I told you," she said. "You aren't alone."

"You don't owe me anything, Layna."

"I know. This isn't about owing you. This is about getting you through."

"I didn't help you get through."

"And I didn't help you. But that was then. And we're both here now."

He wanted to tell her he didn't need any help getting through, but the words stuck in his throat. "What do we do exactly? He isn't awake."

"Talk to him."

"I would feel stupid."

"King Stephanos."

She approached the bed, small and regal. Yes, it was she who belonged in this position while he…he was not sure he had a place in life much less in Kyonos.

"It's Layna Xenakos. And I'm here with Xander. He's home. He's here for you. For Kyonos."

She turned back to face him and the sun caught in her hair, catching the deep golds that were woven in with the browns. She was practically glowing, and he had a feeling he couldn't even blame the sun. She seemed to glow from the inside. "I don't feel silly."

"No," he said. "I can see that. But it's been longer since I talked to him so…"

"Yeah, like a week longer." She reached out and grabbed his arm, squeezed it. "I understand, though. I know you left on poor terms."

"Understatement there."

He looked at his father and tried to find one part of himself there. Because part of him had always hoped his mother had been wrong. But he could see nothing of himself in the old man. Eva's stubborn chin, so many of Stavros's features. But nothing of himself.

The king wasn't his father.

He'd never for a moment believed his mother would lie about his parentage, but he had hoped off and on that she might be mistaken. Denial was a beautiful state. The one he chose to live in.

Suddenly, the room seemed too small. The beeping machines all too loud and antiseptic burned his nose. "Let's go," he said, undoing the top button on his shirt. Damn. He couldn't breathe. "I have to go."

He pushed through the curtain and out into the halls, gasping for air. It was a luxurious environment for a medical center. The sort of place you sent kings, of course. But no matter how comfortable, it couldn't ease him now.

He walked down the hall with long strides, pushed open the doors and went out to the parking lot, leaning forward with his hands on his knees.

"What happened, Xander? I know he looks sick...he's your father and..."

"No...Layna..." He couldn't say it. He could barely think it. He could barely think at all. So instead he did what felt right. And it felt right to take her arm and pull her up against him.

He stroked her cheek—the undamaged side—and he really couldn't see the point in holding back on what he wanted. Not now. Not when everything felt terrible and he just wanted to lose himself again.

Before he'd run. From Kyonos. From himself.

He couldn't do that now.

And there was only one other way he could think of to lose himself completely.

He leaned down and took her mouth. And he wasn't gentle. Because this wasn't for her. Madonna or whore, it didn't matter to him, all that mattered was the feel of her lips on his and what it did for him.

And oh, *Theos*, what it did.

It set him on fire. The flames so hot he could feel nothing else. Nothing but his desire. Nothing but this. He coaxed her lips open, sliding his tongue against hers as he delved in deep.

Yes. This was what he needed. He could drown in this. In her sweetness. She didn't know how to kiss him back, her rhythm a step behind his, her fingers curled into the front of his shirt like little claws.

And it was the most wholly erotic kiss he'd ever experienced in his life.

"Where is the car?" he asked, feeling beyond himself. Unable to think straight.

"Over...over there," she said.

He took her hand and led her over to the limo, which was parked near the front doors. He must have passed it on his way out of the building. He honestly couldn't remember it, though.

He jerked open the back door and got in, pulling her in with him, reaching across and closing the door behind him, with her half on his chest, her leg draped over his lap.

She had no makeup on today. Her dark hair was loose around her face, and she was back in one of those unflattering dresses. He needed to take her shopping. But he had no time to concern himself with that. Not now. Not when her touch, her lips, were so perfect.

He made sure the divider between them and

their driver was up, and then he pulled her to him, kissing her deeper, harder than he'd done outside. He poured everything into the kiss. All of his anger. All of his desire. Everything.

He breathed her in, and he found he wasn't suffocating anymore.

He could forget himself like this. Because a woman like her would never kiss a man like him and that meant that it was easy to pretend he was different. A different man, in a different time and place.

But he knew it was Layna. He knew it when he cupped her cheek and brushed a thumb over her rough scars. When he lightened the pressure on her lips and felt the hardened tissue by one corner of her mouth with his tongue.

Layna, who the media called ugly. Layna, who he wanted more than anything. To possess, to protect. He wanted all of it. Everything.

He put his hands on her hips, bunched the thin fabric of her dress into his fists and pushed it upward. Her body was a treasure. Full, round hips, a slim waist and those breasts…the ones that had haunted his dreams since he'd seen them in that gown of hers.

He needed to see her again. All of her. Now.

He pushed her dress up farther and she pulled back, breathing heavily, her eyes wide. "What are you doing?"

"If you have to ask, clearly I've done something wrong." He was so hard it hurt. And his lungs felt tight now. Being deprived of her lips was like being deprived of oxygen. He needed her. He couldn't explain it, but he did.

But he would never let her know.

She shifted and moved away from him, tucking her hair behind her ear. "I mean, I know you were…that you were…"

"That I was about to make love to you?"

"Well, that. But we're in a parking lot. Our driver is just behind that divider and I seriously doubt these windows are that tinted."

He frowned and looked outside. "There's no one around."

Layna felt like she'd been underwater for too long. Her lungs were burning, her head was fuzzy and her body ached. Though it ached in very pointed and telling places. How was she supposed to think when he was kissing her like that?

He'd essentially devoured her. In a parking lot.

She'd never been devoured by a man in her life, much less had it happen while she was in a parking lot.

It was scary, how he managed to steal her control, her common sense. How he made her lose sight of everything. That they were in public, that she was inexperienced. That she'd been about two minutes away from losing her virginity in the back of a limo.

Yes, he made her lose sight of a lot of things.

But when he'd run out of the medical building, his pain had been palpable. Coming off him in waves, a deep hurt that she knew he wouldn't share. One she knew he'd had to exhaust by kissing her. For some reason.

"It doesn't matter that there's no one around. People don't just…do that."

"I do," he said. His posture readjusted. To this sort of slouched position in the seat, a half smile on his face. Gone was the desperate man of a moment before, replaced by the Xander character that he was so very fond of playing.

"Well, I don't. So that's something you'll have to deal with being married to me."

"You're a prude?" he asked.

"Practically a nun," she answered.

"*Touché.*" He straightened and pushed the intercom button that fed into the front half of the limo. "Back to the palace, please."

"Are you going to tell me what happened back there?"

"It's not important."

"You can just tell me that you aren't going to tell me. It's more honest than saying it's not important. Don't say things that affect you that deeply aren't important."

"Well, it's unimportant in terms of you and I."

"I see."

"You can't act like a miffed fiancée, Layna, not when you don't act like a fiancée when I need you to."

She frowned and looked at him, ignoring the kick in her heartbeat. "What do you mean by that?"

"If you were my real fiancée, and by that I mean, if you were with me for some reason that extended beyond the desire to heal the country and protect them from my wickedness," he said, his tone dry, "then you would have lifted your dress for me and given me the thing I really needed."

"What is that supposed to mean?" she asked, her voice tight.

"That it wasn't talking I needed, baby. It was f—"

"Stop it," she said. "Stop turning into a horrible...beast every time you encounter territory that wounds you. Whatever happened between you and your father isn't my fault. In fact, I've suffered enough due to all of those events, thank you."

"Why don't you take a little pleasure out of it?"

"Can we stop? Can we stop with this shallow, ridiculous nonsense. You aren't telling me what's really going on. And I'm not going to let you... not here."

"Still sticking with your wedding night plan?" he asked.

"Yes." Although it was more for self-protection now than anything else. To prove that she could wait. To prove she wasn't helpless against this thing. This...this attraction.

"Then I suppose we won't have much need of each other over the next few weeks. What I would like you to do is coordinate with Athena, my father's personal assistant. She has all of the information regarding Kyonos, the budget, various charities and so on. Make that your project. And I'm going to be sending you a new wardrobe. You're not allowed to turn it away. Burn those dresses you've been wearing."

"I'm donating them," she sniffed, irritated by his high-handedness. But she wasn't about to argue because what he was proposing meant that she got to avoid him.

"Do as you like, but you aren't wearing them anymore."

"No, I have a better idea," she said. "For every one outfit purchased for me, two new outfits—new—will be donated to a battered women's shelter."

"That is your affair, not mine."

"If I'm going to get something out of this arrangement I intend to start now."

He looked at her, dark eyes molten, and an answering heat started in her core. She knew challenging him was a bad idea. But she didn't really care. Something about him made her feel free. Made her feel like she could say anything. Made her feel like she was no longer bound up by a bunch of safe parameters.

She wasn't sure she liked it at all. Though, goading Xander had its merits.

"I will make sure you get something out of this marriage, *agape mou*," he said, his voice rough. "Several times a night if you're a very good girl."

Her cheeks heated. The bastard. "Perhaps I will endeavor to be a bad girl then."

A slow smile curved his lips. "Even better."

True to his word, Xander avoided her over the course of the next two weeks. And she kept busy. Athena had a lot of useful information and between the two of them, they had endless ideas for more efficient and helpful social programs and ways to help fund various charities.

It was the big picture of all she'd done at the convent. There, she'd been on the ground, physically handing out clothing and food, and it had been wonderfully rewarding. But this was like flying over Kyonos in a helicopter, being able to see every bit of it at once.

And even better because she had the resources to help.

The sad thing was, though, that she was unhappy not seeing Xander. Darn him. She should be glad to get a reprieve. And yet she wasn't.

She'd grown accustomed to his presence. To not feeling alone.

She missed riding. She would have to do something about that eventually, but she'd honestly been so busy. But then, she supposed that was the trade-off. Going from a life of service, reflection and meditation, to a life of high-octane service, balls and luncheons.

There were ever so many luncheons and she'd been invited to all of them. But people were shockingly nice to her.

It made her feel like she might be able to weather it after all. And the makeup artist Xander had hired to help her get ready for big public events didn't hurt. Neither did the new wardrobe that suited her figure so nicely.

She managed to look polished at the very least.

She glanced into the dining room and saw Xander sitting at the table, an expression of doom on his face, papers spread out in front of him. Her heart jolted. She hadn't run into him at all in days, and there he was, just sitting there.

"Hello," she said, coming into the room. She

wasn't going to avoid him. He was her fiancé after all, and it would be silly.

He pushed the papers together, stacking them oddly, his frown intensifying. "I would have thought you'd be ensconced in an office with Athena."

"We're done for the day. Athena had to go home and see to her sick child. Why are you glaring daggers at the headlines?"

"It is nothing," he said, waving his hand. "Just… the news is never good, is it?"

"I don't know. I've spent so much time cut off from it." She wandered over to where he was sitting and he shifted his elbow, like he was trying to hide something from her view.

Buried beneath the top pages, she saw the edge of what looked like her dress from the ball. "What is this?"

"It is nothing," he repeated.

"Then I can see it." She reached down and jerked the paper from beneath the stack and his arm, holding it up, her stomach sinking as she saw the headline and the accompanying photo. "The Zombie Princess," she said. "Oh."

"I will not have this," he said, his tone dark. "I will take steps to make it stop. I'll…"

"Abolish the freedom of the press?" she asked, feeling dizzy. "There's nothing you can do. They… they can think what they want and write what they want. After all. It's only…it's nothing. Vanity."

"You told me to stop pretending like the things weren't important." He took the paper back from her, throwing it down on the table.

"Yes, well, you didn't follow my advice, did you? Why should I follow yours?"

"Because this is garbage. They've hurt you. And I will not allow this to continue."

"It's clever. A joke. An old one. Because I look a little undead. All things considered there were worse things to be called, though."

"Name one."

She put shaking hands on her hips. "I…I can't think of any but it doesn't mean they don't exist. It could be Zombie Drudge, so…you know…Princess is better than that."

"I didn't want this," he said.

She took a deep breath. "I know. And now it's happened. The press did what I thought they would do. They took the easy route and insulted my looks. But that's not actually very surprising. It's what they do. It's how they operate. I can't exactly get upset about it." As she said it, a tear slid down her cheek. "Ignore that. I don't know why that happened."

Except she did. It was like being pulled from her shell, a defenseless crustacean exposed to the elements and scrubbed raw by the sand. This whole experience had been like that. Being with Xander, being back in the world. She'd lost her protection and it left her feeling wounded and fragile.

"Bastards." He picked up his cell phone and dialed a number. "This is Xander Drakos. I want you to track down the owner of *National Daily News* and let him know that if he likes his pants, he'd better print a retraction for his recent article featuring my fiancée. Otherwise, I'll sue them off of him." He hung up. "There. I feel better, I don't know about you."

"It wasn't necessary."

"Oh, come on, there's no point in having power if you don't abuse it a little."

"I take back what I said about you being perfect for the job," she said.

Xander stood, looking down at her, his dark

eyes intense. For a moment she thought he might pull her into his arms. Thought he might kiss her again like he'd done yesterday. And she found she wanted him to.

"Can I see the rest of the article?"

"Why?"

"Please."

He handed the paper back to her and she skimmed the article. One thing that had changed about the tone of the articles was the way the press seemed to see Xander. He was being hailed as a man who had changed. As evidenced by his will-ingness to marry her.

"Well, they seem happier with you," she said. "That's good."

"Is it?"

"It's what you wanted."

"They seem to think I've reformed," he said.

"Have you?"

"I'm not sure."

"Are you going to run again?" she asked, arms crossed under her breasts, her chin tilted up, de-fiant. If he was, he'd better tell her now.

"No."

"Then you won't screw it up. Because I don't

think it's in you to fail. You have to walk away from everything entirely in order to slack off last time."

"I'm not going to run permanently," he said slowly, "but I might need a day off. Do you want to come with me?"

"Where?" she asked.

"The beach. I think I need a day at the beach."

For the beach drive, Xander chose that ostentatious sports car rather than the limo. This moment really did feel like it was from another time. Strangely light. Strangely happy. The Zombie Princess headline lingered in the background, but right now, the mountains were green and beautiful and the beach was a glittering jewel. The windows were rolled down and the wind whipped through the car, smelling of salt and sand and sun.

"Now, this reminds me of the past," she said. "But in a good way."

"Me, too," he said, looking over at her briefly before putting his focus back on the road.

"There's that little window of life where you don't worry about much of anything. I think being seventeen was my favorite. I could drive and could do things I wanted with friends. But I wasn't quite to my dynastic engagement with you, so there was nothing too serious happening. Just parties and trips to the beach."

"I never had that. I mean, I was always raised to be the heir."

"You always seemed happy, though. Like you were having fun at life's expense."

"Yeah, well, I sort of was at that point. I always knew my responsibility, but I liked to have fun. Because, that's the flip side of the heir responsibility. I was assured of my place. Of my divine right to become the most powerful man on the island. How can a young guy not get off on that?"

"I suppose it's impossible."

They rounded a corner and she noticed Xander's knuckles get white on the wheel. She looked up at him, at the hard expression on his face.

"What?" she asked.

"Nothing." She could see his chest, rising and falling hard and fast as he struggled to breathe.

"What's happening, Xander?"

"I'm so stupid," he said, his lips white as his knuckles now. "I didn't realize where I was going."

She really thought he might pass out on her now.

"Pull over," she said. "Just up here, there's a place with beach access."

He nodded slowly and pulled the car into a gravel turn-out on the side of the road, killing the engine. There was silence except for the sound of his breathing and the crashing of the waves.

"What happened?" she asked.

He got out of the car without saying anything, the keys in the ignition, the door open. And he started down the stairs that led down to the beach.

And all she could do was stare after him.

She wondered what pain hurt so bad that he couldn't bring himself to speak about it. It was related to what had happened to him yesterday with his father, she was sure of that. She unbuckled and got out, following him down to the beach, white sand sifting into her sandals, piling into a warm ball beneath the arch of her foot. She kicked the shoes off and ran ahead to where he was.

He started walking into the ocean. She remembered telling him how she'd longed to do that. To disappear beneath the waves and never come back up. And then he dipped his head beneath the water, and Layna couldn't see him anymore.

CHAPTER ELEVEN

"Xander!" Layna shouted, following him out into the waves.

The waves were hitting her at chest level. She gave up on walking and tried to tread water, even though she could touch the bottom. But the waves washed her backward, away from him. "Xander!" she sputtered, water going over her head. She let the water draw her back toward the shore and stood hip-deep in the surf.

He came back up then, his dark head breaking the surface. A wave pushed him back so that he was near her.

"Are you trying to drown yourself?" she asked, feeling half-drowned herself. She knew all the beautiful makeup that had been put on in an effort to de-zombiefy her was gone.

"No," he said, his words heavy. "Not that. Just... I felt like there was blood all over my hands and I thought maybe I could get them clean."

She moved closer to him and took his hands in hers. And without asking why, without asking for an account of his sins, she held his hand up. "I don't see any."

"It's there."

"Tell me," she said.

"I couldn't go any further," he said. "I'm sorry."

"Don't apologize to me. Explain. Explain all of it. Yesterday, today. Something hurts badly enough that you have to run when it catches up with you and I want to know what it is."

"We were going to have to pass the accident site to get to the beach I had in mind and for some reason I didn't realize until we went around that last corner. It reminded me of that day."

"Oh…no, Xander I'm sorry."

"I'm sure it's horrible to watch someone die," he said, a shiver racking his body, "even if they're a stranger. But to watch your mother…to watch her get white, all of her color bleeding out of her, onto your hands…there is nothing worse." He met her gaze, the demons behind his eyes raging now, lashing him from the inside out. "I couldn't do anything but sit with her until help arrived and by then it was too late. But they couldn't get me to let go of her. The last thing she ever heard from me was anger. Those were the last sounds she heard on this earth. Me yelling at her. Swearing at her. I was...so angry with her, Layna."

"About what?"

"It doesn't matter," he said. "It doesn't change anything. It doesn't change what happened. It doesn't change the last moments of that relationship. I can never fix it. Can never apologize for the words I said. I can never go back and decide not to get angry. Decide to pull the car over. Decide not to go out that day. I can never go back and tell her that no matter how angry I was back then, I would have gotten over it and we would have been okay."

He shivered again. "Get on the sand," she said, "out of the water, and wait for me."

She scrambled back up the stairs, up to where the car was parked and took the keys from the ignition, fished a blanket and food out of the trunk, then closed all the doors before heading back down to where he sat.

She threw the blanket over his shoulders. "There. And I have sandwiches."

"I don't think I could eat," he said.

"Then we'll talk."

"Trust me?" he asked.

"Not really."

"Probably a good thing. But if memory from my misspent youth serves me, there's a cave over here. We could get out of the wind. And not have anyone stumble across the heir to the throne shivering and on the cusp of a mental breakdown."

"That might be for the best."

He kept the blanket on his shoulders and led the way down the beach and away from the water.

"This is all a little too perfect, Xander," she said, walking into the small stone alcove cut into the mountain.

"My break with reality and emotional meltdown?"

"How many women have you seduced in here?"

"Oh, this was my much younger misspent youth. Not my teenage years."

"I never really knew if you'd dated much before we were together."

He winced. "I didn't date so much as take advantage of women who liked the idea of getting dirty with a prince."

"I see."

"I take it you didn't?"

She blushed, but thankfully, in the dark she knew he couldn't see it. "I come from a political family and my mother was very blunt with me early on about what nets you a good husband. Purity, or at the very least the illusion of it, is quite important. Princes and the like don't want a lot of tabloid articles going around about their future wife's wild years."

He laughed. "I was expertly snared, wasn't I?"

"We both knew what our marriage was supposed to be. But yes, I did work to make my image one that would fit in with the Drakos family. I worked to be suitable."

"You did far too much for me," he said. "I never deserved any of it."

"I didn't do it for you," she said. "I did it for me. I don't think you fully grasp what a shallow little power grabber I was."

"You were far too pretty for me to care."

"Yes, and when life took that I had to work on developing my character a bit. A harsh wake-up call, and I resisted it for as long as I could."

"I'm still resisting it," he said. He put his hand

on the rough stone wall and looked up. "I know a little bit about those hazy years, you know."

"Do you?" she asked, her throat tight all of a sudden.

"Yes. I was so high for the first couple of years after I left I could barely remember my reason for taking off in the first place. It was a lot harder to remember what it was like washing my mother's blood off of my body, too."

"It's terrible to live like that," she said. "Half alive."

"I tried to use things like sex and drugs to make myself feel. But in the end, it doesn't work. It's fleeting and the aftermath is so bad you wish you would have just stuck with empty."

"When did you stop?"

"The drugs? Probably twelve years ago. The drinking and sleeping around? It's been a couple of weeks. I've been walking with my favorite crutches for a long time."

"It's funny. I've been in a convent and you've been in a casino, but I think, at the end of the day we were doing the same thing."

"I think you might be right."

"I'm sorry about what happened. And I'm sorry

I was so angry at you. I didn't really stop and think about how you must have felt. All you must have gone through. My own tragedy overshadowed yours in my mind."

"I don't blame you for that, Layna. You were put through hell."

"We both were."

"Yesterday when I kissed you," he said, "I just wanted to lose myself. To forget who I was. Where I was. To forget that this was my life. That my father, who I haven't spoken to in so long, was unconscious. That he's dying. Another person I'll never reconcile with. When I kiss you it's hard to think about any of the bad things because…I just want you."

"Kissing me really works that well?"

"Yes," he said.

"The Zombie Princess?"

"I don't have time for people like that. They're idiots. They don't know what it's like to kiss your lips, or feel your curves beneath their hands. They know nothing."

She was really blushing now. "It's hard for me to think when we kiss, too. I didn't think I would miss touch. I thought I could live without being with a man because I didn't want to deal with the fact that I could be rejected for my looks. Or that any man who was with me might be with me out of pity. But when you kiss me, I care less about how you feel because I'm too focused on what I feel."

"I make you selfish?" he asked, moving closer to her.

"Yes. For that. For what you can give me. I've… never actually been kissed by anyone else. And the one thing I always regretted, in spite of myself, was that the night in the garden, you know what night I mean, we got interrupted."

"I regretted that, too. I tried not to think of you after I left, Layna, but I did regret that. I regretted you. If my life hadn't have changed, you would have been my future, and I was always content with that vision. The life I've had has never been as beautiful as that dream. As that certainty I had for those few months we were engaged. I could see it all, you as my wife, us ruling Kyonos, and it felt right. Maybe that was really why I came to look for you after I returned. Because I hoped that somehow it wouldn't be too late to have some of that."

"And look what you came back to."

He put his hand on her cheek, a move he made often and one she didn't think she'd ever tire of. He was so comfortable touching her, even her scars. "But the feelings are the same. It's amazing how much we've both changed, only to come back to this point." He put his hand on her other cheek and lowered his head, kissing her, deep and long. "I do want you. As badly as I ever have. More even, I think, because I know how bitterly I've regretted the fact that I didn't claim you before. I will never make that mistake again."

She looked up into his eyes. They were still so bleak, so haunted. She could see it even in the dim light of the cave. "Do you need me?" she asked. "Do you need to forget?"

She did. She was wounded and hurting. For her, for him. For everything they'd lost. For the years of pain. For the years they suffered alone when maybe what they should have done was cling to each other.

"Yes," he said. "Please."

She kissed him then. Slowly traced the seam of his mouth with her tongue, asking for entry. He gave it, and with a growl wrapped his arms around her waist and held her tightly against him as he let her take the lead on the kiss.

She knew she was a little clumsy at it, but he really didn't seem to mind, his erection hard against her stomach, an air of desperation coming from him in waves.

She could feel it reflected in her, deep in her core. The need to feel like she wasn't alone. He'd said that he'd been inside of a woman before and felt utterly isolated, but somehow she knew that wouldn't be true with them.

Because they both knew rock bottom. And it seemed like they deserved to reach for the heights, even if it was just for a few moments.

He took the blanket off his shoulders and laid it down on the sandy floor of the cave. "I have never seduced a woman in here before," he said. "I know I told you that already but it feels like my current actions might make that assertion seem suspect."

"A little bit, but I don't really care," she said, blinking back tears. "I've been cold for a long time," she said.

"Because you were in the ocean."

She laughed and shook her head. "No, I've been

cold inside for a long time. I feel like you could make me warm. I need you to make me warm."

"You deserve better than this," he said, kissing her again, cutting off any response she might have made. "You deserve so much better than this, but I don't have the strength to give it to you, because all I can do is take this for myself."

His desperation fed hers, the need that wrapped itself around his voice was like balm for the scars inside. She might be the Zombie Princess, but right then, the beautiful, damaged prince wanted her.

They were both broken. Barely limping through life. But maybe if they held on to each other tight enough they could hold each other up. Maybe she could be strong enough if they were braced on each other.

He swept his hand over the line of her back, a wave of sensation crashing over her. How long had it been since she'd focused on her body? On what she felt physically. She'd been training herself to deny physical desire. To deny cravings of any kind. Of specific foods, rest, sex. Because it was important for a woman with her aims to deny herself.

But right now, Xander was making it impossible to think of anything else except what she felt. What she wanted. He was making her need, a deep, aching need that she couldn't possibly let go unanswered.

She wouldn't let it go unanswered. She knew what he meant now. Because she knew what she should do, too. She knew she should ask for a bed and soft sheets, and for him to be slow and gentle because it was her first time.

She knew she should demand marriage vows, because it was right.

But she was beyond that. None of it mattered. The cave floor would do, the commitment they had would have to as well.

She had a feeling that, if she had met him again and he hadn't offered marriage, they would be in the exact same position.

Because this was unfinished business. This was the chance to either bond her and Xander together for good, or to at least have him lose some of his power over her by answering some very important questions. The chance to turn regrets of missed chances into mistakes made.

She was honestly okay with the idea that it might

be a mistake when it was over. Because she was short on those. Or maybe not. Maybe her life had been one long, steady, low-key mistake.

That sent a jolt of panic through her, spurred her on, made her kiss him all the more desperately. Xander made her feel so much. So many things she thought she'd let go of, and he brought it all roaring back, or to life for the very first time.

He pushed his hands beneath her shirt, repeating his earlier move, this time over bare skin. She moved her hands to his stomach, tugging his shirt out from his pants and slipping her fingers beneath. He was so hot, so hard. So very different from her.

She would have been shocked by her boldness in other circumstances. But not now. Not when they were in the dark. In this place that almost seemed removed from reality. Not when they were holding each other up.

Not when they were helping each other forget by filling the present with so much pleasure the past couldn't exist anymore, and the future couldn't be a concern.

He pulled his lips from hers and kissed her neck, teeth grazing her sensitive skin, his tongue sliding over her flesh to soothe away the sting. He knew just where to hit, just when to stop and suck at her skin, when to inflict pain. When to give pleasure.

He tightened his hold on her and drew her forward, raising his other hand to cup her breast through the fabric of her damp top. He moved his thumb, finding her nipple with ease, finishing the work of the cold water and tightening it to a painfully hard point.

A low growl rolled through his throat and he propelled her backward, pushing her against the wall of the cave. He pushed a thigh between her legs, then took advantage of her widened stance, his arousal coming into contact with the most intimate part of her.

There were layers of clothing between them but she still felt it, so devastating. So erotic. So unlike anything she'd given herself permission to want or feel for far too long.

She'd told him that she was a woman, and had been long before he'd walked back into her life. And it was true. But she'd suppressed an amazing part of what it meant to be a woman, and only now, with his lips on her skin, his hands on her body, his hardness against her softness, did she realize that.

She angled her head and caught his lips, kissing him deep, tasting him, reveling in the slide of his tongue against hers. For too long she'd had hazy. Gentle. Life on a near flat line with barely a blip, and now she felt like she was going to explode with the intensity of this encounter. With the rawness of it.

The rock at her back, the man at her front, the sound of the waves just outside the cave walls. It was sensory overload in the most perfect way. An infusion of sensation, bursts of flavor on her tongue. Years of bread and water dissolving into a sensual feast that she didn't think she would ever get enough of.

He forked his fingers through her hair and tugged, hard, guiding her away from the wall, down onto the blanket, his body covering hers, his lean hips settling between her legs. She bucked against him, chasing the promise of release that sparked through her with every touch of his body against hers.

He pushed her dress up, tugged her panties down to her knees, his hand at the apex of her thighs, thumb deftly finding the sensitive bud there. She didn't have time to be shocked or embarrassed, didn't have time to do anything but simply revel in the pleasure he knew how to give.

"You want me," he said, his voice feral, his words barely intelligible.

"Yes," she said, kissing his neck. "Yes."

The blanket was bunched up underneath them, only offering a partial shield between them and the ground, but she didn't care. It added to the intensity, to the depth of it all.

He slipped a finger inside of her and the wholly foreign sensation rocketed her to the brink of orgasm.

"You're a virgin, aren't you?" he asked, his voice hoarse.

"Yes," she said, pleasure rocketing through her as he slid his thumb over her clitoris again.

"And you're sure this is what you want?"

"I need it," she said. "I need you. I need it like this."

"It's not going to be romantic," he said, abandoning her body, reaching for the closure on his pants and unbuttoning them, then tugging his shirt over his head. "It's probably going to be fast."

"Are you trying to talk me out of it?"

"*Theos*, yes. Because if I have a soul left, this will damn it for sure."

She shook her head. "No. It won't. How could that be true? How can that be true when I feel like if I don't have you I'll die?"

He kissed her lips, gentle, searching, at odds with the ferocity of the moment. "That's absolute proof that I'm right," he said. "I'll try not to hurt you."

The blunt head of him probed at the entrance to her body and she tensed for a second before he started to push inside. The farther in he went, the more she relaxed. It didn't hurt. It just felt…new. And wonderful.

He put his hand under her bottom and lifted it, thrusting into her all the way. A harsh sound escaped from his lips, along with a curse that sounded more like a prayer.

He pushed her dress up higher, exposing her breasts, lowering his head and sucking a nipple deep in his mouth as he moved inside of her, driving her higher, faster than she'd imagined possible.

It seemed natural, having him like this, moving with him, finding her pace. She locked her legs around his lean hips and arched against him, meeting his every thrust, nails digging into his shoulders.

He lowered his head, his movements harder, faster now, pleasure sparking in her, each thrust bringing the bursts of white heat closer together, turning it into a continuous flame that burned through her whole body, threatening to consume her as he ravaged her, pushed her to a point she hadn't imagined possible.

Xander growled, teeth closing down on her shoulder, his pelvis hitting hard as he froze above her and shuddered out his release. The pain ramped her pleasure up higher, the overflow of sensation an utter shock. Beautiful. Blinding.

And when the fire burned out, it was only the sound of their breathing echoing off the walls of the cave.

A chill stole through her blood, a slow trickle of ice that replaced the heat that had come before. And it hit her that she was lying on the floor, outdoors, kind of, almost, with Xander on top of her.

Her dress was still on, his pants only pushed down just past his hips. That she'd let him—no, begged him—to take her like this. When they weren't married. When they hardly knew each other. When they certainly didn't love each other.

He moved off her, standing and tugging his pants up, his movements fluid as he dressed. It all spoke of his experience—experience he'd gained with other women.

Anger curled in the pit of her stomach. Anger she had no right to feel because she knew his past, she knew something of his experiences, and she'd just benefitted, mightily, from those experiences. It had been…amazing. Physically.

Emotionally she felt…an empty, crushing weight in her chest. The kind he'd spoken of. They'd just been as close as two people could possibly be and she felt alone. More alone than she'd felt in ages, with him right there, the scent of his skin still on her body. It made no sense.

Sex without love.

Yes, that had to be it. Lust. Empty lust that meant nothing.

But it had all seemed substantial in the moment. It had seemed necessary. Now she felt singed inside. Like she'd been burned, hollowed out.

No wonder she'd spent so many years content

with…contentment. Happy to feel no brilliant highs so that she could avoid the lows. So that she could avoid this level of emptiness and confusion.

"Let's not talk," she said, scrambling into a sitting position and trying to put her clothes back in place. "Let's just…not."

"Why?" he asked, doing his belt and the final few buttons on his shirt.

"Because there's no point. I don't want to…I don't want."

"Do you regret it?"

"I don't understand it."

"What's not to understand? We wanted each other. We acted on it."

"Didn't I just say I don't want to talk?"

"Hiding?"

"Why not?" she asked, feeling like she was on the verge of tears. "It's what we're both best at. We hide from our pain and our issues and from anyone who might hurt us or ask anything from us, right?"

"Sums it up," he said, his tone hard. "And that right there is my favorite method of running. You have to admit, it's a lot more exciting than hiding in a convent."

"It was more *something*, but I haven't decided if I liked it or not yet."

He grabbed her arm and pulled her forward, kissed her hard on the mouth. "You liked it."

"I did?" she asked, keeping her voice monotone.

"You came pretty hard, baby, you can't hide that from me. I could feel it."

Her face heated. "Don't."

"Don't because you want to pretend that you're just a sweet, good girl? We both know you aren't."

"That's where you're wrong, Xander. Assuming I care about being good. I don't. I never have. I just cared about hiding. I've never needed to be good, and I think if I had, I wouldn't have given you my virginity on the floor of a cave."

"Then maybe our marriage will be a success, *agape*, because if neither of us care about being good, then we might have a lot of fun."

"More fun like that, you mean?" she asked, her tone disdainful.

"Yes," he said, "that's exactly what I mean." He hauled her against him for a kiss, his lips hard on hers. "And don't play wounded maiden with me. It doesn't suit you."

"What? All my wounds aren't convincing enough for you?"

He released his hold on her. "Whatever the hell your problem is? Get over it. I expect sex in my marriage and since you don't want me to have it with anyone else, I'll damn sure have it with you. Unlike you, running off into celibacy isn't my style."

"You are...you are..."

"Sexy?"

"Your ego is..."

"Yeah, I know. But I don't need ego in this instance. I know just how much you enjoyed that, so let's just skip this part."

She gritted her teeth. "I believe I'm the one who suggested that in the first place."

"So we'll continue with it then."

Layna dressed, careful not to look at Xander as she did, then headed out of the cave and into the sunlight. It was shocking that it was still midday. Shocking that the world seemed so normal outside while everything inside of her was rearranged to the point where she couldn't find a damn thing!

And, yes, damn again. She blamed Xander for her expanding vocabulary. Not that she hadn't known the words, just that she hadn't seen fit to use them until he'd come back into her life.

"For what it's worth," Xander said, his voice coming from behind her, "I do feel better."

"I think I might find that offensive."

"Don't," he said. "Because usually I feel worse when it's over, and I don't. Even after we've had a fight. Actually, I think I like that we had a fight."

"Why?" she asked, incredulous now.

"Because we talked. And I don't want to leave it on a fight because sometimes, you never get a chance to repair it when it's over."

Her heart squeezed. "I suppose that's true."

"A truce, then?"

She didn't really know how she felt about a truce with the man she'd just had sex with. She didn't know how she felt at all.

He stuck his hand out, as though she was meant to shake it and all she could do was stare. "A truce?" she repeated, sounding dumb.

"It's better than fighting, don't you think?"

But not very honest. Not when she felt all jumbled up. "Okay." She extended her hand and wrapped her fingers around his, shaking it slowly. This was silly, but it meant she was able to stop and collect herself. Shore up her defenses. It meant neither of them had to be particularly honest.

She was quite comfortable with that.

"Good," he said, releasing his hold on her. "Now, let's go. I think we both agree that a day at the beach has been had and there's no need to go any further."

No need for him to pass the site of his mother's accident. No need for them to confront what had passed between them. No need for them to talk about why he felt so dirty. Why he'd felt the need to walk into the ocean to get clean.

"Yes," she said. "I think I'm quite ready to go back."

He smiled, and she knew that he knew, as well as she did, what they were both doing.

Hiding.

"Excellent."

CHAPTER TWELVE

XANDER COULDN'T GET his tie right. And who the hell cared? He hated all of this. Hated that he had to dress for dinner because Stavros had invited heads of state and all other manner of dignitaries Xander could care less about.

Not when he was highly concerned with his feelings for his fiancée. Or rather, how his fiancée had felt when she'd been naked underneath him. Being with her yesterday had been a revelation. He swore succinctly and tossed his tie down onto the bed.

She had been… There were no words for the blinding flash of perfect oblivion and clarity he'd found when he'd pushed inside her body.

And wasn't that a damned funny thing? He'd always known sex had power. It had the power to wipe his worries from his mind. The power to make him feel. To bring his life, the emptiness of it, into sharp perspective the moment the buzz from his orgasm faded.

But this was different. He hadn't felt alone when he'd been with her.

Maybe it was because they were both so very much the same, though he doubted she would ever admit to that.

He looked down at the tie and frowned. Then picked it up.

He could call a servant, but he hated that nonsense. He probably needed a valet or some such, no doubt his father had one.

But that wouldn't serve his purposes for the moment. Sure, it would get his tie on straight, but it wouldn't serve his purposes.

He flung his bedroom door open and stalked down the corridor. The servants were very good at ignoring him and his moods. But then, he supposed that was part of earning their salary.

He opened the door to Layna's room without knocking, hoping he might find her there. He was not disappointed.

"I need help," he said, his tone as stern as the walk he'd used to bring him here.

Layna frowned from her position on the bed.

"You have a very bad habit of barging into my room."

"Since when does a fiancé need permission? And I have now seen all of your body, so let's not even pretend that your modesty is offended."

"Just because you've seen it once doesn't mean you have ongoing permission to see it whenever you like," she said.

"Of course it does." He sat down in a chair by the bed, one leg out straight, his arms on the rests. "I am to be king. I will see what I like when I like to see it."

She arched her brows. "Has being in your childhood home caused this regression or do you just always behave like a recalcitrant boy?"

"I need help putting my tie on," he growled. He was not going to dignify her question with a response.

"Then why didn't you call someone?"

"What the hell is the point of a wife who doesn't want me to see her naked and who won't tie my damned tie for me?"

"I'm not really sure, actually. Maybe it's the time for you to rethink your proposal."

"I won't." He stood up and walked toward her, draping his tie over his shoulders. "Fix this."

She let out a long, exasperated breath and gripped both ends of the tie. "It's been about a million years since I've done this. I did it for my father a couple of times. He felt it would be a good skill to know."

"For such a time as this, I should think."

"Clearly, yes, the idea was for me to be able to serve the every whim of my crabby husband. But you are not my husband yet, don't forget it."

"I made you mine in every way that counted today."

"Indeed," she said, her tone frosty.

"You don't agree?"

"Does every woman you have sex with belong to you? If so, we should start partitioning off a wing for the royal harem."

He pulled away from her and started working on the tie on his own again. "You need to dress for dinner."

"And the subject has changed."

"It bloody well has."

"Are you always such a horror after sex?"

"No, but I am always such a horror when I have

to put on a tie and perform at some…state dinner I have no desire to partake in."

"So I should expect a lot of this then?"

He sat down again, his hands folded, his chin braced on his knuckles. "I have to get over it, don't I?"

"What?"

"The fact that I don't like this. Or want it. That I don't know how to do it anymore."

"How is it that you managed to lose all of what you were raised for? How did you lose so much of who you were born to be?"

Xander shifted in his seat. And he wondered if it was time she knew. "Because it's not who I was born to be."

It was too late to take it back now. There was no pulling back from a statement like that. She would never let him off the hook now.

"What do you mean?" she asked.

It didn't mean he wouldn't make her drag it out of him since just saying it seemed too hard.

"The way the system works here in Kyonos, it's almost as if our bloodline gives us some divine ruling powers. I mean, Stavros's children can't be in line for the throne because they're adopted, because they don't descend from our great and noble lineage. Are there magic powers in it, I wonder? I've always wondered that, even when I was a boy. Wondered how I'd been so fortunate to be born with such blood and the divine right to rule that came with it."

"No wonder you were so insufferable."

"Yes, it's no wonder at all when you're born believing that the simple act of your birth puts you above the common folks." He took a breath and looked out the window, at the slice of blue sky just barely visible. Not for the first time, he thought he would rather sail into the horizon than deal with all of this. But he'd made a promise.

He'd made a promise to Layna.

He wouldn't run again.

"But I found out…that I was not born with that right at all. I have no royal blood, Layna. I am not my father's son."

"What?" He had succeeded in shocking her. Her eyes flew wide, one eyebrow raised, the other, paralyzed by scar tissue, still managing to convey her surprise.

"That was what my mother and I were fighting about. She told me, on our trip to the beach that day that I was not of royal blood, but the product of an affair she had with her bodyguard. Ironic, considering Eva's marriage. But my sister had the courage to walk away from her arranged marriage when she decided Mak was the one she wanted. My mother made a different choice. She went ahead with the marriage to my father, knowing she was pregnant."

"What? How…"

"She seduced him quickly, is my understanding, and it was no hardship to convince him I was born just a few weeks early."

"But she's certain?"

"So she told me. She was already pregnant when she slept with my father for the first time."

"And the bodyguard?"

"Sent away with a grand payoff. She never took a test of any kind, and that was, in the end, why she told me."

"What do you mean?"

"She'd been getting increasingly paranoid, with the way technology was progressing. She was starting to fear that someday my DNA might be used against me. And so she begged me not to ever undergo any sort of analysis of my blood. Or to ever let my children undergo such a test, when you and I were married."

"But why would she…?"

"I think it was long-held guilt, starting to eat at her, making her see shadows where there were none. But the thing was, the economy had been having issues already and with the state of political unrest she was concerned for me."

"But if… Why couldn't Stavros rule then?"

"My father didn't know. She didn't want him to know. She loved him by then, you see? She hadn't loved him when they'd first married. So lying to him hadn't seemed so bad. But later… she wanted to keep it a secret. For her. For him. And for me. In her mind, I was her firstborn son and I deserved the honor. I think in some ways, I was her favorite son because of my real father. Because he was her first love. Because she had gone to such great lengths to protect me and ensure I was the heir."

He shrugged.

"I've had fifteen years to think this over. And I have. High, drunk, sober, alone and in the arms of a woman, I've thought about this. About what it meant. About what my responsibilities were.

She did so much to ensure I could be named the heir. But the fact remains that I'm not."

"And that's why you left?"

"That. And the fact that I do blame myself for her death. I was so angry, Layna. I could hardly see straight and I was yelling, I just drove faster and..."

"You made a mistake. You didn't do it on purpose."

He shook his head. "I didn't. But it was a hell of a mistake. There are mistakes you can come back from, but then there are mistakes you make that someone doesn't walk away from, and those are the hardest ones to deal with. The hardest ones to seek forgiveness for. From yourself or anyone else."

"Tell me about the day you left," she said, sinking to the floor in front of him. "Tell me about what happened, now that I know everything."

"My father had called me into his office. Stavros was there, too." He could picture them both—his father ashen, angry and grieving. His brother, so young and sullen. A teenage boy still. "And then he proceeded to tell me that he found me responsible for the death of his wife. And how he had no idea how I could possibly be his son, when he would never have behaved in such a manner. And I had no argument. For I felt he spoke the truth. And I had just learned I was not his son. So there was no lie in what he said."

"And Stavros?"

Xander cleared his throat. He hated that the memory had this much power over him, even now.

"He looked at me and said he would always hold me responsible for the loss of his mother. His mother, as though she were no longer mine because I had taken her from the world. And remembering the words I'd yelled at her before the car hit the rocks? Where I had said she was no longer a mother to me? I couldn't argue with that statement, either."

"And you had nothing," she said, her voice a whisper.

"In one moment, I lost all my family. And I knew I had no real claim on the throne. I saw no reason to stay."

She rose up, planting her hands on his thighs, and kissed him on the mouth, the touch sweet, sincere. He raised his hands and gripped the back of her head, his fingers sinking deep into her hair, holding her tight to his mouth. He needed this. He needed her. He needed her so badly he was shaking with it already and it had been less than twenty-four hours since he'd last been inside her body.

He tugged gently on her hair, tilting her head back, exposing her tender throat, then he lowered his head and kissed her, slowly. She moaned, encouraging him, spurring him on. He bared his teeth, scraped her delicate skin and reveled in the raw sound she made in response.

She liked this. His little innocent. She liked him unrestrained. She liked to be at his mercy. Which naturally put him at hers. To have a woman on her knees before him, allowing him this kind of sensual feast? He might have the physical power, but she was holding the leash.

Keeping his hand in her hair, he reached down to his belt and undid the buckle, freeing himself from the confines of his pants.

She looked up at him, angelic eyes wide, her lips in a shocked *O*. There was something about that face that turned him on even more, and it shouldn't. He knew it shouldn't.

"You know what I want from you?" he asked, his voice strangled.

She nodded slowly and he tightened his hold on her hair. He watched the color in her cheeks rise, from arousal, not embarrassment. The flush spread down to her neck, her chest.

"Suck me," he said, his voice rough.

She leaned forward, guided by his hand, the tip of her tongue touching his rigid length.

"More," he said, tugging gently.

But she didn't comply. Instead, she just ran her tongue along his shaft. And he could do nothing but sit helplessly, let her have her way. She shifted then, taking all of him into her mouth, and he leaned back in the chair, a harsh breath hissing out through his teeth.

He swore, short and to the point, but it only seemed to encourage her. She wasn't shy. She seemed to have no qualms about tasting him, touching him, boldly changing the rhythm or stopping altogether, squeezing the base of him with her hand, pushing him to the brink.

"Careful," he groaned, when her tongue brushed the sensitive skin just beneath the head of his erection. "I don't want it like this. I don't want it over too soon."

The look she gave him was wicked, reminding him of Layna Xenakos as she had been. Confident. A minx. A flirt. A woman who had a sensual air about her, and an innocence, too. It had all called to him even then.

She had always called to him.

She lowered her head again and he tugged her hair. "No," he said, his voice sharp. "I want to be inside you."

She stood then, lifting her dress and tugging her panties off. He reached for her, hooked his arm around her waist and tugged her onto his lap, bunching her dress up around her hips, squeezing her bare butt before giving her an open-handed slap. Nothing too hard. Just enough to draw one of those sweet sounds from her lips.

Then he gripped her hips tight and positioned her over his body, testing her with the blunt head of him, finding her wet and ready. He starting to pull her down, sliding into her by inches. Her head fell back and he couldn't resist another nip on her throat.

When he was inside her all the way, she rested

her head against his chest, her hands on his shoulders. "Yes, Xander," she said, and he knew she was still with him.

A relief, because he'd been so lost in his own need it would have been easy to forget her. To forget that she might not be ready for this. But she was. She was right there with him.

"My dress," she said, panting, "would you—?"

He tugged it up higher, pulling it over her head and throwing it to the floor, then undoing her bra with unmatched speed, exposing her breasts. "My pleasure," he said, lowering his head and sucking one rosy bud between his lips.

She arched against him, her internal muscles flexing around him. It was too much for him. But he'd already taken too much from this and she needed hers. He needed to watch her face as she came for him.

He reached between them, sliding his thumb over her clitoris as he thrust up into her.

Her fingernails dug into his back and for a moment she lost herself. But he didn't lose her. He held her the whole time. Watched as her lips parted, her eyes closed, her forehead creased. The way the scar tissue by the corner of her mouth folded, and how one brow never did match up with the other.

It was all her. No one else could have made this moment. No one else could have coaxed his darkest secret from him and then taken him to heaven on its wings.

She squeezed him tight, and the world exploded, his blood turning to fire and swallowing him whole while his orgasm burned through him, clearing out all the pain, all the regret, all of who he was and who he'd been, leaving him desolate in its wake.

And when he came back to himself, he was in her arms. And he wasn't sure who he was. Or why he'd cared so much about a tie only a few minutes ago.

"When is dinner?" she asked, her voice sleepy.

"Eight," he said.

"So we have five hours," she said.

He nodded and somehow, in spite of the fact that his legs felt like jelly, he managed to lift them both from the chair and carry her to the bed. He pulled back the covers and laid her down, then got in beside her, pulling her body up against his. He buried his face in her hair and took a deep breath, the air filling his lungs seeming all the fresher because it was infused with her scent.

"I should have done this after the first time," he said.

"What?"

"Taken you to bed. Held you close. You're so soft." He let his hand drift over her curves. Her hip, her thigh. "You are beautiful, Layna. I saw it just now. With that look on your face as you came. The most beautiful thing I've ever seen."

"You don't have to say those kinds of things."

"I know. But it's true. And you asked me only last week if I could say you were beautiful, and I said no. But I was wrong then. I know so much more now."

"A week to obtain wisdom. I wish I had that gift."

"Not wisdom in all things. But wisdom in how magical it is to watch you lose yourself in pleasure. To see the light catch your hair and pick up the hidden gold strands that always remind me of the past. Only the good parts of the past," he said, laughing. "And I don't know quite how I missed just what an incredible thing your smile is. Because you still have it. Because life has been cruel to you and you still smile."

"So do you," she said.

"Yes. But you mean it."

"You don't?"

He shook his head. "I already told you. I think we took different paths to accomplish the same goal. I tried to pretend everything was fine. I hid behind my smile. Behind artificial highs. So that I could pretend I felt something when I simply didn't. When I couldn't go back and face all that I needed to face. The only thing to do was never look at the past, and pretend everything was fine in the present."

He felt her nod, her body shifting slightly against his. "Yes. That sounds about right. I mean, I understand that."

"And you?"

"In my case, I thought if I could focus on other things, not myself, for a while, I would be okay. If I could have some purpose beyond living in a darkened mansion floating around like a tragic, gothic heroine, then maybe none of it would hurt so bad."

"Did it work?" he asked.

"Yeah. It did. I…I love helping people. And I was able to surround myself with women who had no love for clothing or fashion. I lived a life where outer beauty was a trap because it could lead to vanity. To pride. And since I had none…" She laughed. "In an odd way I suppose I soothed my pride that way. Because I was clearly the least in terms of looks, so I was starting at a greater advantage, and I could be proud of that. That it wasn't a challenge for me to avoid the mirror or to not long to spend ages on my appearance. So…I guess what I really did was try to find a new place I could be the best. But I wasn't that good at it to be honest. I had—I *have* faith. I believe. But I preferred to ride horses and not meditate indoors. I love food, and it was always hard to fast. But it was quiet. And easy to be content and nothing more. Nothing less."

"You always use that word to describe it," he said. "You never say happy. Content is the one."

"Because happiness is too big, I guess. Unlike you, Xander, I haven't been searching for the big emotional high. A return to feeling. It hurts too much to lose everything. And if you care…if you care then it's almost impossible to recover from.

Not only did I lose everything, I had an audience. And the moment when I was attacked I had no control. I just stood there. Screaming and screaming, the pain…I can't even describe the pain."

He felt a tear splash onto his arm and an answering ache echoed in his chest.

"And I just let them all have it. Every drop of it. The protesters, the media, everyone. I never want to be like that again. I never want to feel so much. But I think…I think just having contentment doesn't work, either."

"You don't think?"

"I was starting to feel a little dry. Brittle. Does that make sense?"

"Like you needed to be watered," he said. "Like you would fade to nothing if you didn't have something new and fresh added to you."

"Yes."

"It makes sense, because I felt it, too." Nothing was real or substantial in his world, nothing truly passionate in hers. And for people like them, it was a recipe for death.

"I think that's why I like the way you are with me," she said, turning her face into his arm, muffling her words.

Heat assaulted his face. A strange thing. Almost like he was embarrassed, which was ridiculous. "The way I am with you?"

"Yes. The way that you're...rough. I know this isn't how it is for everyone. I understand that the way I like it isn't the way everyone does."

"No," he said, his blood rushing south, "it's not."

"But I think the reason it works for me is that I spent so long filled with nothing but this sort of bland steadiness. And you... You fill me with sensation. Pleasure and pain so sweet I can't bear it. It lifts me up from contentment and takes me somewhere else entirely." She turned over to face him, her expression serious. "But it's only physical, so it feels safe. Does that make sense?"

"Yes," he said, ignoring the uncomfortable tightness in his lungs. "Yes, that makes sense."

"I don't shock you, do I?"

He had to laugh at that. "You shock me? Until yesterday you were a thirty-three-year-old virgin fresh from the c—"

"Convent, I know," she said, sighing, sounding exasperated. "But look at it this way: I've had a lot of years of nothing more than fantasy. A lot of...desire building up inside me and all. And it was sort of by accident I discovered I liked a bit of rough. I blame the cave wall."

"Do you?"

"And you. I think you're corrupting me."

He laughed again, but this time not because it was particularly funny. "I'm afraid that might actually be true."

"I'm happy with it." She shifted against him. "So, what are you going to do?"

"About?"

"You aren't the heir."

"I know," he said. "And for years I was deciding to just not be the heir, but Stavros's circumstances and Eva's wishes have changed that for me."

"I understand that."

"But you don't approve?" he asked.

"It's not that I don't approve. It's just that I wonder if your father needs to know. If your family needs to know."

He tightened his hold on her. "I can't do that."

"Why not? Because you might lose your place?"

"Because I might…I won't have…"

"You won't have your family."

The tension released from him slowly. He was

glad she'd said it and not him. "Silly, I know, considering I hadn't spoken to any of them in ages."

"But they were there. I understand that. My family is there, even though we don't really speak."

"Why is that, Layna?"

"It's easier not to. For all of us. I should think you would understand that."

"I do."

"Why don't we sleep for a while," she said, yawning. "Then…then maybe I'll do better tying your tie, and we'll have a hope of being on time for dinner."

CHAPTER THIRTEEN

THE PLAN TO make it to dinner perfectly pressed and on time didn't exactly go off without a hitch. Halfway through tying Xander's tie for the second time, Layna found herself tangled up in him, and the bedsheets, again.

That put them behind schedule by a good twenty minutes, and by then, she hadn't been able to have her makeup artist coat her face with all the paint she needed to begin to cover her scars, which meant she was rocking a much more natural look for the dinner than she'd intended.

But Xander didn't seem to mind.

And he'd called her beautiful.

Something bloomed inside of her, like a flower that had found the sun after a long battle with the clouds. And she wanted badly to crush it herself. But she couldn't bring herself to do it.

It was frightening, how much his words meant to her, and yet she found she wanted to hold them close, even knowing that doing that might be too costly.

She didn't know how today had happened. All that nudity, and not just in bed. It had been real honesty that had passed between them.

And their lovemaking was… She felt her cheeks heat even as they walked into the dining room together, where ten dignitaries were already seated. Yes, their lovemaking was explosive and far beyond anything she'd ever imagined.

If she thought way back to when she'd imagined she might have a sexual relationship with a man, then she remembered having fantasies about Xander. But she remembered them as being quite calm and hazy. Certainly not with her loving the bite of pain from his hands in her hair and rough demands issued from his lips.

She tried to look casual as the past few hours replayed in her mind. This was not the time. This was a formal dinner. Stavros and Jessica were seated near Eva and Mak, and the head of the table was empty, as was the foot. And just like it was choreographed, she and Xander parted and he walked up to his chair, while she moved down to hers.

It was choreographed, she supposed. From a time long passed, but even so, they both knew the steps. They were steps ingrained in them from years ago. It was the position they'd trained for. The marriage they'd trained for.

So strange to be here now, after she'd let go of it all. So strange to have it be so much the same to what she'd imagined and also so different.

They both had scars now. They had the kind of passion that had nothing to do with a bored, disinterested worldview. They might even be better people now than when they'd first been poised to slip into this roll.

"In the absence of my father," Xander said, "I will be acting as host."

"And how is the king?" One of the politicians to Xander's right posed the question.

"He is as well as can be expected. I would hope he makes a recovery."

"But of course we can't plan for that," Eva said, looking bleak.

"We can't plan for the worst, either, Eva," Xander said. "We can prepare for it, but why not do that and then plan on a better outcome?"

She smiled. "I like that idea better than mine. I tend to be a catastrophist."

"I think this family has had enough catastrophes," he said.

Layna looked down the table at Stavros, who was looking at his older brother with an expression that was…almost like approval. It made her heart do strange and wonderful things. Because she found that she cared about what happened with Xander and his family. It made her ache for him. Made her appreciate how truly difficult things were for him.

Because he felt like he had a smaller foothold on the Drakos family than he should. Because he wasn't truly a Drakos at all, but the child of an unnamed man he would never know.

It made her want to go to him. Made her want to hold his hand. But that wasn't the proper thing to do. So she would help him by being everything a royal wife should be. She wasn't his wife yet, but today she was acting the part. It was what she could do for him, so she would do it.

The conversation turned to unchallenging things. No one questioned Xander on his years away, no one asked about her scars. No one compared her to a zombie. All in all it went very well.

And when it was over, Xander, Stavros and Mak adjourned to Xander's study—and it killed Layna not to follow and act as support—while Eva and Jessica stayed behind with her.

"We can take coffee in my study," she said, gesturing for them to follow her. She felt like a bit of a fraud considering Eva had lived in the palace until a couple of years ago, and Jessica was a frequent guest, where Layna was just learning the layout of everything.

Both women smiled graciously and followed her, and Layna waited until they were seated before settling herself in one of the armchairs that was positioned by the fireplace. It was lit and roaring already. She was used to having to see to things like that herself. But she wasn't going to complain.

"He's doing well," Jessica said.

Eva smiled, a kind of special smile a little sister has for her older brother. "He's brilliant."

"And both of you are happy?" Layna asked. "With the order of things, I mean. Jessica, I understand that when you married Stavros it was with the idea that he would rule. That you would—"

Jessica shifted in her seat, her red lips pursed. "Neither of us have ever really wanted it. He would have done it, because he believes so strongly in doing his duty. But he loves his business, and frankly, I love mine."

"Are you still a matchmaker then?" Layna asked, having been briefed on her future sister-in-law already.

"Yes. We both work less now that we have the children. Lucy and Ella take up a lot of time, after all, but we're both still heavily committed to the companies we've built. Stavros is so interested in bringing more business to Kyonos and he's thrilled to have more time to focus on that. And more flexibility for the girls. It would have been a hard life for them. Raised with the strictures of being the king and queen's daughters, with no hope of ever taking the throne. They would be considered second forever, because of their blood." Jessica's eyes glittered in the firelight. "The idea of that…I can't stand it. I'm so glad they were spared it. I had no idea how hard it would be until we were faced with the reality of what it would mean for them."

"I hadn't thought of that, either," Layna said, looking down at her hands. "How terrible it would be for them." And Xander, how terrible it would have been for him. To be the oldest child in the household and not be the heir. In some households, the matter of blood could be forgotten because love forged the bond. But in a royal house it was different. In a royal house blood was so much more important.

She swallowed and looked up at Eva. "And you, Eva? What about your children? Do you want this for them?"

Eva shook her head. "I've always chafed at what was expected of me. I don't see why my children would be any different."

"And Eva would be bored with palace life," Jessica said. "It's no wonder she had no desire to marry a prince."

Eva smiled. "Or perhaps I just liked what the bodyguard had on offer."

Jessica winked broadly and crossed her legs, her tulle skirt fanning out around her. "The prince does all right."

"Thanks, Jess."

"Oh, come on. Don't get prudish on me now, Eva. You didn't get that baby bump by eating a watermelon seed."

Eva sniffed. "How very American of you."

Layna laughed, genuinely enjoying the interplay between the two women. Between these women who would now be her family. And it was a relief to her to hear they didn't want the throne anywhere near them.

"Yep. I'm totally American like that. Another reason I probably shouldn't be the queen of anything," Jessica said.

It all made Layna appreciate the impossible place Xander was in even more. The reason he'd run. The reason everything had felt so hopeless.

It wasn't enough to have your father look you in the eye and lay the blame for your mother's death on you. He'd had to experience it knowing that the man wasn't really his father. That there was no magical bond between them. Not a blood bond.

And in a family like this, blood was everything.

"How about you, Layna?" Eva asked. "Are you all right with being in this position?"

"There is nothing holding me to the position. Nothing forcing my hand."

"Except for your relationship with Xander," Jessica said, her eyes narrowed.

She and Xander did have a relationship now, and she couldn't deny it. Not after they'd been together so intimately. Not when she felt this need to protect him.

"Xander and I have an understanding, based on our desire to see the country succeed. It has always been our goal. We were just derailed for a while."

The back of her neck prickled and she looked up—Xander was standing the doorway.

"Forgive me if I'm interrupting. But I'm ready to retire. I had thought you might come with me, Layna?"

There was something strange in his eyes. A raw, wounded look that she could see behind the careful facade he had in place.

She always saw through those walls, and sometimes, she wished she didn't.

Sometimes she wished she could go back to simplifying him. To not seeing him. Or at least to seeing him as nothing more than a playboy.

Now she saw all of his wounds. Now she saw he was just as scarred as she was and it made it hard for her to hold onto her anger. Hard to keep her shields up.

And she needed her shields. Because when they were down, it burned like acid. And she knew, better than anyone, just how that felt.

Because she couldn't deny him now, even if she should. Even if they needed distance from today so that she could make sure she felt shored up again.

But she couldn't deny him. And she wouldn't.

"Of course, Xander." She stood and looked back at Eva and Jessica, who were giving her saucy raised eyebrows. She wanted to tell them it wasn't what they thought. Except it was what they thought and she knew it. Xander needed her, and if he needed her, it would be her body he required.

And she would give it.

She made her way to the door and took his arm, allowing him to lead her up the stairs and down the winding corridors until they were at his bedchamber.

"I had a maid send your things," he said. "I

didn't see any point in pretending things weren't like this between us."

"Of course not."

He started to undo his tie, the one she had done earlier. It was a strange thing, to be a part of both rituals. The dressing and the undressing.

It made things feel very serious.

"I suppose you want—" She was going to say "sex" but he sat on the edge of the bed on a heavy sigh that seemed to demand silence.

Then he tented his fingers in front of his face, staring sightlessly ahead. "I feel like it's wrong not to tell them."

He wanted to talk? That really did shock her. More than that, it wasn't what she wanted. It was too much. Too challenging.

"Maybe you should think on it. You'll feel better after—" Again, she was going to say "sex," but he pressed on.

"Stavros is well-suited to the position. Listening to his thoughts on the economy I found myself quite humbled. I am not uneducated in these matters, but he's a man who has examined the way things function on every level. From the workforce to the day-to-day running of things. Stockholders and traders, different kinds of industry. He's truly a man now and not the boy I often see him as. He makes me feel like the stupid boy, to be honest. He's been here holding everything up while I've been..." He paused and looked down. "Layna, I've done less than nothing. I didn't even have the decency to get employed somewhere, I gambled for room and board. And Mak...he's not royal and yet he's got a core of steel. Nothing would ever break him. His children, his and Eva's, would be well-suited to taking the throne one day."

"But they don't want it," she said.

He nodded slowly. "I know it. And I find myself in an impossible situation where I feel I must become a better man to make up for the fact that Stavros won't be the one on the throne, and I don't know how to be better."

Her heart ached, her throat tightening. This was too much. He was making her feel too much. Not in the delicious pleasure-pain way that came through sex. This was all in her heart. A heart she'd kept protected for so long that every lash of emotion felt like being hit with a battering ram.

"It doesn't seem like something we can solve

tonight. Maybe we can—" She was going to say "have sex," but this time he cut her off with a kiss. And when he swept her into his arms, and into bed, she could focus on that.

On the sensations he created on her skin, not beneath it. The smooth and sensual, the rough and hard. And she let it all fill her. Until she was conscious of nothing more. Until the pain in her heart was overshadowed with sweeter physical pain, and much sweeter physical pleasure.

And when it was over, they didn't talk. They held each other until they fell asleep.

Layna's last thought before drifting off was that it was very strange not to be alone.

This was the second time in his life that Xander Drakos had woken up with a woman in his bed. The first time had been the previous afternoon, when he and Layna had napped after their pretty intense sex session.

And now, here it was, morning. He'd slept with her all night long, with her curves pressed up against him, his arms tight around her. Very tight. Like he was afraid she might escape.

But she wouldn't. Layna was so constant. So faithful.

If anyone could teach him how to be a better man, it was her. She didn't have royal blood and she was the epitome of steadiness and temperance. Well, maybe not really. But she did a wonderful job of acting like she was and maybe that was enough.

All he'd had practice at was indulging his more selfish whims.

Layna had spent years denying hers.

Perhaps he could learn something about restraint from her.

He shifted and looked down at the top of her head, at the golden highlights he could see, revealed by the shaft of sunlight breaking through the drapes.

"Layna," he said.

"What?" she mumbled sleepily. She wiggled against him then startled, drawing back to look at him, blinking like a mole who'd just come out of her burrow. "I forgot you would be here. Or that I would be here. With you."

"I was quite surprised to wake up with someone myself, but I find I don't mind it."

"You've slept with lots of women," she said.

"I've had sex with a lot of women," he said, heat bleeding over his cheekbones. "I don't sleep with them."

"Oh. Well."

"They never mind. They're usually staying in the same hotel."

"That's right. I forgot you didn't have a home."

"And if I had, I wouldn't have brought them to it."

"You are quite something, you know?" she asked.

"That's the thing, Layna, I do know, which leads me to what I was going to ask you."

"Which is?"

"Make me better."

"What?"

"I need to be…better. I have to be able to justify the fact that I'm the one taking the throne and not Stavros."

"No," she said, "you don't. You don't have to justify anything. Not to me. I talked to Jessica and Eva last night and they explained very clearly why they don't want it differently. Eva doesn't want her children raised in this environment and Jessica can't stand the idea of her husband being king while his children can't inherit because they're adopted. There. You're absolved."

"No, Layna, I'm not. Because that's not what ruling is. It's not being comfortable or making everyone happy. It's doing what's best. Stavros knows this. He would accept it if I were to leave."

"You said you wouldn't run," she said. Not accusing, just a fact.

"Is it running if you're simply trying to protect your country? Your people."

"What is it you need to do to feel like a better man?"

"I guess it's too late for me to join the church."

She blinked. "A bit. If you still plan on marrying me."

If he left, he would have no reason to marry her. Which drove home the point that he had to stay. Whatever happened. She was too important to him, and he didn't want to stop and examine why.

But she was changing him. Just being near her was changing him, and he needed that. Needed to be with her. Otherwise, what was there? Nothing more than that endless haze of neon lights and booze. And the idea of going back there now felt like the equivalent of walking into hell of his own free will.

He held her tighter. "And I am planning on it," he said. "You have my ring and my word."

"I've had both before."

"The man I was," he said. "Not the man I am now. And I'm vowing to change."

"So you'll stay."

"Yes. And does it matter to you so much that I do?"

She frowned. "I want you to have a place in the world, Xander. Everyone should. I don't want you to go back to the life that you were living. I don't want you separated from your family."

"And you tell me, since I imagine you know more about this than either of us, where is truth in all of this?"

"I don't know, Xander. Maybe there is no place for it."

"Seems like that might be heresy."

"Maybe. But isn't all of this? Life dealt us both an impossible hand. We either fold or we cheat. I'm becoming convinced of that."

"A gambling metaphor. You know me so well."

"Well, you were asking about the church, I thought I'd bring in the casino."

"Since we're aiming for heresy?"

She sat up, the blankets clutched to her chest. "Not exactly aiming for it." She pushed her hair off of her face.

She didn't seem so self-conscious of her scars around him anymore, and he found he quite liked that.

Especially since he didn't see them the same way he had at first. When he'd first seen them they'd looked like they weren't real. Like they were a mask over the face he remembered. Now it wasn't that way. He saw them as a part of her face. They didn't bear extra notice, not more than those mesmerizing eyes, or the shape of her nose. The stubborn set of her chin.

They weren't an intruder on his eyes or on her beauty. They were a part of who she was, what she'd been through.

Sometimes looking at them hurt, because it was a reminder of how much she'd been hurt. It was a reminder of her pain. But also a reminder of her strength.

"You're staring," she said, her eyes narrowing.

"Because I like to look at you." He let his eyes

drift down lower. "But I do wish you'd drop the sheet. I could compose poetry about your breasts. And I don't even like poetry."

She surprised him by letting the sheet fall to her waist, her full, rose-tipped breasts on display for him.

He smiled. "Damn. I'm glad to be a man."

"That's the best you have, Drakos?"

"Shall I compare your nipples to a summer's day?"

"Okay, you can stop now."

"I don't think I can. Not ever."

She let out a long breath. "Xander, I don't know what I'm going to do with you."

Stay with me.

It was the first thought in his mind. It was the thing he wanted above all else.

"Reform me," he said, his throat tight.

"Sometimes," she said, looking away from him, "I'm not really sure I want you reformed."

He pulled her close and kissed her for that. And then more. Until everything faded away. And when they were done, Xander wasn't alone anymore. He was with Layna. And he felt it all the way through.

248 PRETENDER TO THE THRONE

And he had never felt more alive. He had never felt more.

"Actually, Xander," she said, her voice a whisper, "I think you're already the best man I've ever known. You make me…you know you make me feel like I just might be…beautiful."

Light burst through him, bringing pain along with it. Like the sun hitting his face after a night of hard drinking. Only this didn't feel like stale regret. It was hope. It was something bigger, better than he'd ever known before. He didn't want to hide. He wanted to push off all the layers of rock and dirt, everything he used to hide himself, his secrets, from the world, to protect himself from the painful truths in his life, and emerge the man he was supposed to be.

But he could never do it, so long as everything was covered. He could never be free until he cut the ropes that bound him in the darkness.

With Layna by his side, the idea of it didn't seem so impossible.

"I have to tell him."

Layna looked up from her lunch and at Xander,

a strange sense of dread filling her chest. "You what?"

"I have to tell him."

And she didn't ask who or what, because she knew. Somehow she knew what he was thinking without him saying it.

"But why, Xander?"

"Because he's my father. Or, he thinks he is, and for all intents and purposes and everything that matters to me, he is. And moreover he's the king, and he has the right to choose who his successor is. With all of the information given to him."

"Xander, don't do this. He won't have a choice—"

"There is always a choice, Layna, and this is the thing I've been hiding from. It was horrible to lose my mother, but I couldn't fight against my father's anger, I couldn't stay because I was far too afraid that the truth would come out and then things would be…then they could never be fixed. I have to tell him everything, all of it. So that I can have forgiveness. So that I can have my life. So I can be free."

"But, Xander," she said, a desperate fear clawing at her now and she didn't know why. Didn't know why this was so terrifying. Only that it was making her feel like she was clinging to the ledge of a cliff, her hold slipping with each passing moment. "If you do this, he might send you away. He might…you might never be king. You won't even be a prince. You'll be the royal bastard."

"I'm the royal bastard whether anyone knows it or not," he said, his voice quiet. "And I can't keep hiding behind a lie. Because that's the key, I think. To reforming. To…to changing and being a man who's actually worth something. I have to stop hiding. And that doesn't mean leaving Monaco and returning to Kyonos, clearly I've done that already."

"It means taking less than you deserve because you've had a sudden attack of conscience," she said, shocked at the words coming out of her own mouth. Shocked at the vehemence behind them. She didn't know why she cared so much. Why it felt so vital and frightening.

"I can't argue with you about this."

"Why not?"

"Because I can't change my mind."

"You're just running," she said, anger and fear

swirling in her and making her panicky. "You're running again."

"No, Layna. I've finally stopped."

Xander got up from his seat at the table and walked out of the room.

His father was awake this time when he went to see him.

"Xander?"

"I suppose you didn't hear that I was back," Xander said, standing in the doorway.

His father lifted a hand. Strange to see King Stephanos like this. So diminished and pale. But he was awake. Perhaps he would recover. Then, at least, the need for Xander, or Stavros to rule wouldn't be so pressing.

Then, at least, he might have some time left with this man. Time he'd wasted in fear.

"Are you back?" his father asked, adjusting his position in the hospital bed, fiddling with the lines from his IV.

"Yes. I am. But...and I know that this is a bad time to drop bombshells on you...."

"Xander, from where I'm sitting, there may be no time. I'm only glad you're here."

"You seem better," Xander said.

He nodded. "Better. I can speak again. Though it took a while. It was a bad stroke."

"I know."

"So say what you need to," he said, "and then I'll tell you what I need to say."

Xander took a breath. "It's about me. And mother."

King Stephanos closed his eyes and nodded. "Yes, we need to talk about that."

"Not the things you might think. There was a reason for the crash. And that is that we were fighting, and I was reckless."

"Xander..."

"No, I need to finish. It was my fault, but I could never truly explain it to you. Not when the circumstances...not when I felt I couldn't tell you the truth of the matter. It seems cruel to tell you now, and if it weren't for the way things work in our family, if it weren't for the importance of royal blood, I wouldn't. I found out that day that I am not your son. She was certain of it."

King Stephanos nodded slowly. "I had suspected, of course. You were born quite early and yet quite healthy."

"You suspected?"

"Yes. But I was hardly going to accuse my new bride of faithless behavior. In truth, Xander, ours was a marriage of convenience. In the beginning. I do think we grew to love each other very much."

Xander nodded. "She did love you."

"There is no reason to condemn her for a sin that's thirty-seven years old."

"I'm afraid I didn't feel that way at the time."

"Of course you didn't. How could you?"

"You understand now why I had to leave," Xander said.

"You had to leave because of me," the king said, his voice heavy with regret. "I was hurting and I said things to you… I was not a loving father."

"But you aren't my father at all," Xander said.

King Stephanos frowned. "Xander, no matter what, you are my son. No matter the revelations, or the years that have gone by, or angry words that passed between us, you are my son."

Layna hung up the phone, her hands shaking. She had no idea how the reporter had gotten her line here at the palace. No idea why he'd felt the need to call and tell her they were doing a story, why he'd needed to recite the ugly things being written about her.

That they had photos of her, standing on the balcony off of Xander's room in a thin nightgown, her hair pulled back revealing the worst of her scars, no makeup on her face. And that they were publishing the photos.

Does he make love to you in the dark?

That was when she'd hung up. Her fingers had felt numb.

She hated this. Hated the way they were exploiting her. The way it made her feel. At first, she'd helped Xander's reputation, but was she helping him now?

He said he needed her, but when his rule was taken over by gossip about her looks, about their marriage, how would he feel then?

She sat down in her office chair and tried to catch her breath, failing as it dissolved into a sob.

What would happen when he didn't need her anymore? When he knew he didn't? When he could have any woman, why would he want her?

And he'd gone to confess all to his father. If that lost him his spot on the throne…he would never keep her with him. Never.

Despair washed over his as every word, every insult from the media, from now and fifteen years ago, played back through her mind.

Xander might not leave her now, but one day…

She'd survived losing him once. She couldn't do it again.

Xander walked into the palace with a strange, buoyant feeling in his chest. He felt lighter. He felt like he could breathe for the first time in fifteen years. And more than that, this felt like a place he could live. A position he could have.

Because his father, the man who would always claim him as his son, had said that Xander was the man he wanted on the throne.

The truth truly did set you free. Interesting. He wondered if Layna would be amused by his epiphany.

Layna. He needed to see Layna.

He needed to have Layna. With none of his walls between them.

He prowled through the halls and opened her bedroom door. She wasn't in the suite of rooms that were set aside for her. He walked out and continued on, toward the place she was using as her office.

He found her there, sitting behind a desk, staring off into space. She started when the door hit the wall.

And as soon as he saw her, every thought left his head completely. He'd forgotten why he was there. Where he'd just been. He forgot everything.

He could only stare at her, at her eyes, her high cheekbones. The extra fold by her mouth where her scar tissue was thick, a fold that deepened when she tightened her lips, like she was doing now. At her asymmetrical brows and her neat, feminine hands.

At Layna. All the pieces of her that combined to make the woman that had changed him on every level. That had changed him in a fundamental way he could neither name nor deny.

And he needed her. Needed to be close to her, inside of her, right now. Needed to affirm what he was feeling. To have her brand his body with her touch the way that she had branded his soul.

To brand her body, so that she would feel it, too.

"Layna..." His words evaporated on his tongue. He didn't know what to say. Or how to say it.

He knew how to flirt, knew how to throw practiced lines at women and get them into bed for the night. But he'd never learned how to keep a woman with him for two nights, much less forever.

But he had to try. He had to try.

Because he'd gotten everything today—acceptance, forgiveness. And still things didn't feel finished.

"Layna," he began again, "you have been missing from my life every day since I walked away."

"Xander, what are you talking about?"

He went over to the desk and rounded to her side, hauled her up into his arms and kissed her. Then he kissed her cheeks, the damaged corner of her mouth, the winkled line of skin that ran along the bridge of her nose.

He pressed his forehead against hers. "I've been wandering in the desert for fifteen years. I have had no home. No one to call a friend. And I was okay with that because I didn't want anyone to get near me. I came back here, it was supposed to be the promised land, so to speak, and I didn't feel anything. I didn't feel home. Until I saw you."

"Xander, please...don't do that, I don't need it."

"I need to tell you."

"How did your meeting with your father go?"

"That isn't what I need to talk about."

"It's what I need to hear about," she said.

Layna tried to calm the wild beating of her heart, tried to do something to quell the panic that was racing through her. She didn't know what to do with this. With his words, his ferocity and sincerity, with such strength that it burrowed beneath her defenses and started pulling them down. Left her feeling raw and exposed. Reminded her of how it had been to lose it all, all of her control, all of her beauty, in front of hundreds of people.

To care so much and have it all torn away...

Zombie Princess. Does he make love to you in the dark?

She closed her eyes and kissed him. She didn't want to hear him speak anymore. She couldn't hear more, not now. She could do this. They could kiss. They could make love. They could get married and live together and have children, and rule Kyonos.

So long as she could keep pieces of herself hidden, so that if the world ever fell down around her again, she wouldn't be left with nothing.

But she had to keep him from saying things like that. He could touch her skin, but she couldn't let him keep on touching her heart.

She couldn't risk it.

"Layna," he growled, kissing her deeper, longer.

It was working. He was focusing on her body now, his hands roaming over her curves. This was what she needed. This overwhelming tide of physical sensation that only he could make her feel.

Because it blocked out the other feelings. The ones that surrounded her heart and pushed at the walls. The ones that she'd made to protect herself.

When he'd said he was going to talk to his father her world had ended for a moment. When he'd made it clear he was willing to take a step that might end what they were building here, and it had made her feel like the earth had simply run out, and she was standing on the edge of a cliff waiting to fall, she'd known she had to shore up her defenses.

And now he was here, and he was saying things. Romantic things. Things that had nothing to do with sex or convenience or honor, and she couldn't do it. She couldn't handle it.

This she could do. This was all they needed.

He just had to remember that. She would make him remember. That this was good. That it was enough.

"Take me," she begged against his lips. "Hard. Now."

But he didn't obey. He kept kissing her, his lips so tender and sweet it made her ache. She didn't want to ache. She didn't want to care.

She didn't want to love or be loved. She didn't want to care about anything. About whether or not they called her the Zombie Princess, or if Xander thought she was beautiful. If Xander stayed with her forever or only for a few months.

She didn't want to care about any of it.

It was too frightening. It asked too much.

"Stop it," she said, pushing against his chest, pushing him against the back wall. "Stop being gentle. Kiss me like you mean it." Like there was nothing else. Like the press didn't exist. Hard enough that he could made her forget, long enough that she wouldn't be able to breathe. That she might drown in it. In this.

She kissed him again, and she felt his fingers lace through her hair, and he tugged hard, drawing her head back. Yes. This was what she wanted.

"I have to look at you for a moment," he said. "You're lovely." He traced her ruined lips with his thumb, holding her still with his other hand, forked deep in her hair.

She shook her head. "I don't need you to lie."

"It's not a lie. Any man that misses your beauty is a fool."

"He's a man who has eyes, Xander." The whole world had eyes. And they didn't like what they saw.

He kissed her hard, a punishment for her talking back. The kind of kiss she wanted. The kind she reveled in. "You should know this, Layna," he said, his voice rough. "Beauty, the kind on your skin, is terribly vain."

"Inner beauty, Xander? Is that what we're talking about?"

"No. For the love of God, woman, do you honestly believe that a rough patch of skin takes away who you are? Takes away your allure? Your beauty? Your lips…your hair and eyes. *Agape*, they are worthy of any man's praise."

She could feel the cracks in her defenses widening. Could feel herself, her resolve, weakening.

"But I don't need praise," she said. "I need you, here and now."

"Sex is all you want?" he asked, a strange note to his voice.

"Sex and a partnership. Anything else is gratuitous."

He tugged her hair harder, kissed her throat. "I can show you gratuitous if you really want."

"Yes," she said.

He leaned down and picked her up, carrying her over to the desk, which was quite clean—and she had the vague thought that it was a good thing it was—and set her down on top of it, stripping himself of his clothes as quickly as possible. "Take them off," he said to her. "All of them."

And she obeyed. From her position on the desk she stripped off her top, pants, underwear and shoes, and stayed perched on the edge while he positioned himself between her thighs. He braced his hands on her hips and slid slowly, making her aware of every inch of him as he entered her.

He lifted one hand and gripped her chin. "Look at me," he demanded.

"No." She didn't know exactly why, but she couldn't.

"Look at me, Layna," he said, thrusting hard into her.

"Xander, please..."

Her eyes flew to his, shock preventing her from doing anything else. From thinking it through. And the minute she saw him, really saw him, her heart started to feel too big for its cage. She looked down again, squeezing her eyes closed.

"Don't shut me out," he said.

"Xander..."

"I love you."

"No," she said, shaking her head, closing her eyes tighter, a tear tracking down her cheek.

"Layna, I love you." He kept moving inside of her, his thrusts matching the terrified rhythm of her heart, as he drove her to the brink with his body while his words delivered fatal damage to the walls surrounding her heart.

"No. Don't love me. Don't ask me to love you."

He cupped her face and kissed her lips, moving hard and deep within her, his mouth covering hers, swallowing her denial, and the cry of pleasure that followed it as her orgasm crashed over her in a perfect storm of agony and ecstasy.

Just like everything with Xander.

Perfect pleasure. Perfect pain. Perfect misery mingled with joy.

When she came back to herself, his arms were around her, and he was holding her tight against his chest. She realized she was shaking. Sobbing.

Because of him. She pushed away from him.

"Xander, I can't…"

"You don't love me?"

"Why do you think you love me?" she asked, even though she didn't want to know the answer. Didn't want to hear any more. "No. Don't answer that. I can't…I can't breathe, Xander. I can't." She started hunting for her clothes, tugging them on as quickly as possible.

"Why not?"

"I thought I could…" She was gasping now, panicking. "I thought I could do this. But do you know why I cling to my contentment? Because at least if I don't…if I don't love anything, if I'm never excited, or overjoyed, I can't go back to the low place again. If I don't care about my looks then I can't be destroyed when people call me names. If I don't love you I can't fall apart when you leave. I can't fall into depression, and that… fog, Xander, that horrible fog. I won't do it again."

"I'm not going to leave you, Layna," he said, walking forward, gripping her arms. "Ever. I made a promise. And I will keep it."

"You didn't mean it, though. You still went to your father and told him the truth, even though it might mean you would lose this. Lose me…"

"I don't have to be king to have you, but I do need you to be a good man. I need you. You don't understand."

"That's just it! So what happens when you don't need me anymore? And you run."

"You don't trust me at all, do you?"

She wrapped her arms around herself, trying to hold it all, hold herself, together. "I don't trust in anything. Not you…not…"

"God?"

"Don't. You don't know what it's like. Fine if you have a trauma, you just get to run and run. But the rest of us are left with nothing. I couldn't run from my pain, Xander it was in me. And you don't know what that is!"

"Oh, I don't?" he growled. "Because throwing my life away on drugs and drinking and sex wasn't a horrible existence? It was, Layna. It was.

It was every bit as dark, and every bit as rock-bottom."

"I don't suppose you ever thought about killing yourself. Because I did. I thought about it a lot."

"I never thought about it," he said. "I just assumed that running toward death at full speed like I was would eventually amount to it. One day you drink too hard, you take too much of the wrong thing, and you don't wake up again. I was sort of hoping for that day, just too much of a coward to pursue it with any kind of real dedication. Or maybe it was the ties here. But for whatever reason, I didn't. Still, I know that place you're talking about. I know that kind of darkness. But I walked up out of it for real today and I want you to do it, too."

She shook her head. "I can't. I can't do it again, Xander. And I'm sure you think that I'm weak. And maybe I am. But I used up all my strength already and I can't possibly put myself at risk like this again. I can't just...put myself out there. All of me, and risk being pushed down into the darkness again."

Xander looked down at the desk. The desk

where they had just made love. He was still naked. And he didn't seem all that concerned about it.

"My father told me that I was his son. No matter what the paternity test might say." He looked up at her. "He's my father no matter what."

"I'm happy for you. I'm happy for...you don't have to have a wife now, do you? Not one like me. You're accepted and your people love you. And I'm the Zombie Princess. You don't need me, Xander."

He hauled her against his chest, holding her to him. "I *do* need you, Layna."

"No, Xander, you don't. And more than that? I'm starting to hurt things for you. At first...at first maybe people loved you for sticking with me, but now I'm just a burden. An embarrassment. It's going to be...I'll be ridiculed by the world. Kyonos will be."

"Whether the people approve of you, or me, or not. I need you because you are the only woman for me. Because I love you beyond words. Because you have reached down deep inside me and shined a light on the real me. Made me look at myself and see who I am, and who I want to be. Because back when I was a selfish, entitled, wreck of a man, you were the only woman for me, and no matter what life has thrown at me in the meantime, at the end of it all, you're still the only woman for me."

"I can't be the woman for you." She pulled out of his hold, and he let her go. "I can't live like this. With…with the press closing in around me all the time. They took pictures of me, Xander. And a reporter called and…"

"What?"

"He asked if you made love to me in the dark."

"Layna…"

"So even if the people love me. Even if they love you being with me. Even if I don't end up embarrassing the nation I can't…I can't do this to myself. They'll never leave me alone. They'll harass me. Forever. For all of my life and I can't…do it."

"And you don't love me?" he asked, his tone flat.

She shook her head, the walls around her heart strengthening, folding in around it like a concrete blockade. "No."

"I see."

"I'm going to go."

"To your room."

"No. Away from here. Just…away from you."

"You're running?" he asked, his tone even,

deadly. "I thought we agreed we weren't going to do that anymore. I thought we promised."

"No, Xander," she said, her voice a whisper. "You promised. I didn't. I don't want any of this. I don't want to be in the public eye, I don't want to be under scrutiny like this. I don't want your love."

"But you have it. I want you to want it all, Layna, I want you to have it all."

"How dare you?" she screamed, angry now, cracking apart inside. "How dare you take my safety away from me! How dare you pull me from my home, from my quiet life and bring me here! You said we would be partners, you didn't say you would demand my soul."

"Nothing less, *agape*. Because you have mine."

"Well, you don't have mine. And I'm going. Goodbye, Xander. I wish you the best of luck in ruling, and in finding your future queen. She won't be me."

"What can I do?" he asked, a desperate thread in his voice that seemed tied to her heart, squeezing her tight, making it impossible to breathe.

"Show me the future. Show me nothing will happen. Show me that if I choose to want again, to feel again, to need again, that I won't have it all ripped from me. Prove to me you won't leave, you won't cheat. Prove to me that things will be well. Show me. Show me that when you don't need me anymore, when your reputation isn't helped by me, you won't want someone else. You won't regret me."

He ran his hand down his face, looking so impossibly tired, so defeated. "You of little faith," he said, laughing bitterly.

"I don't know how you can say that to me."

"I don't know how you can claim to be anything different. You spend fifteen years in a convent, pretending to be a woman of faith when you don't have enough to feel an emotion that transcends anything more than basic contentment. You're afraid to take a deep breath, Layna Xenakos, afraid to make a ripple for fear God might notice you and strike at you again. Afraid to live."

"I'm not. That's not it…."

"The hell it's not. At least I can do this. At least I can put the past behind me and walk forward. You don't want to go back to that hell you were living in, but you keep one foot in it to remind yourself. You keep yourself afraid. You keep yourself from ever feeling happiness. From ever feeling love. What's the point of protecting yourself if all you're protecting is a life half-lived?"

"Tell me why I should trust you," she spat, "when all your history proves that when things get hard, you'll leave. You haven't earned my faith, so don't stand there and talk about how I don't have it."

He jerked back like he'd been slapped. But he was only stunned for a moment. "I haven't earned your faith?" he asked. "All that I have given you, all that I have promised you, my body, my soul, and I have not earned your faith? Think of what I promised you before I ran the last time. Nothing. Engagements end, which happened with ours. I had not made vows to you, I had not promised undying love. I hadn't even promised you undying lust. I promise it all to you now and then some. I give you my word, my vow, that I will never leave you, no matter what comes. I give you everything I am. I'm laying it at your feet here, Layna. But now you tell me I have not earned your faith."

She looked at him, at his eyes, blazing with anger and hurt, burning inside her so that she had no choice but to look away. Because what she'd said was worthy of anger. Insults he didn't deserve.

She took her ring off. Shaking, she put it in his hand, forcing his fingers to close around it. "This is the second time I've returned a ring to your family. Maybe...maybe don't offer me one again."

"Is that really what you want?" he asked, his voice strained.

She nodded, trying to keep the tears from falling. "Yes. It is."

She walked out of the office and ignored Xander shouting her name. Ignored the sound of his footsteps behind her as she ran to her room. She looked around, at all the pretty things. And decided she didn't need any of it.

She wouldn't stop running again until she'd reached safety. Until she could feel safely hidden from the wall of grief that was threatening to overwhelm her.

CHAPTER FOURTEEN

LAYNA RODE UNTIL her thigh muscles burned and her lungs ached. Across the fields and up to the highest point on the hilltop, where she could look over the ocean. The wind was blowing her hair everywhere, her horse shifting his weight beneath her.

The drunken gambler didn't think she had faith, it would make her laugh if she didn't feel like she was cracking apart inside. Stupid man. Stupid, stupid man.

She closed her eyes and inhaled deeply, the salty air burning her throat. Mother Superior hadn't blinked overly much at her return, but this morning she'd called Layna into her office and told that she would have to make a choice now.

Either she would take her vows, or she would find somewhere else to go. The abbess hadn't been unkind, but the simple fact was, Layna's room had been filled and she'd been off living...well, unchastely. That was the truth and she couldn't deny it.

This wasn't a place for her to hide, while she was free to have bouts of going off and doing what she wanted. It wasn't fair. Or right.

Damn Xander. She had no idea who she was anymore.

You of little faith.

It wasn't fair. He was asking her to have faith in him but she didn't have a guarantee. She couldn't be sure that she wouldn't lose everything again.

That she wouldn't be left stranded at rock bottom alone.

For we walk by faith, not by sight.

Well, that was just inconvenient. She got off her horse and looked out at the ocean, over the rolling, gray waves. Everything seemed to have been leached of color to accommodate her mood and she appreciated it. At least something was working in her favor.

Suddenly she was hit by a wave of sadness so strong it crippled her. She went down to her knees, the moisture from the grass bleeding through her dress.

He was right. She had no faith. It took no faith

to hide. You didn't need faith when you were safe. Didn't need it behind the walls of a convent, where you were protected from the world. When your every need was met daily and you were never challenged, you didn't need faith.

You didn't need faith when you were a novice who'd spent years managing to not take vows. Not taking the leap of faith and committing the trust it took to go wholly into that life, not having the faith to go back into the world and try to live.

She'd condemned herself to a halflife in exchange for safety. It wasn't the press that scared her. It was what he made her feel.

He made her feel so exposed. He didn't accept her excuses. Didn't let her scars keep him at a distance. He wanted it all. Worse, he wanted her to have it all.

And wasn't sure she was brave enough to ever take that risk again.

If ever there was a time Xander wanted to run, it was now. From the searing pain in his chest. From the burning in his eyes, from tears, damn it, and not because he was hung over.

He hadn't had anything to drink since she'd left.

It was like he'd well and truly changed. Fancy that. Change didn't feel all that rewarding when you were sober and you didn't have the woman you loved.

A pain shot through his chest. Yes, he did love her. He wondered now if he always had. If he'd been a shallow boy, in love with a shallow, beautiful girl. Until their world shook apart and he'd gone off licking his wounds.

He'd come back a man changed, to find her a woman changed. And to find that everything that had been there between them from the beginning was still there. That the tragedies of life had reshaped them, so much so that they fit together now even more perfectly than before.

And she was too afraid to see it. Too afraid to reach out and take it. To trust him. To be with him. She was choosing to be unhappy so that she wouldn't be devastated and that killed him.

Unless she just doesn't love you.

Well, that was always a possibility. But still, with him or without him, she was choosing fear over happiness and that ate at him. Because it was what he'd done for so long. Because he was an expert in empty, meaningless things. In pursuits that were vain and useless.

In turning away from everything pure and strong, and hard and wonderful, so that he could simply find some shelter from reality.

He was done with that now, though. He loved her. More than the throne. More than his own life.

So he could sit here and brood soberly, or he could go after her. Make a fool of himself. Again. For her love. And if he couldn't have her love, he would beg her to let go of all that pain and live the life she was meant to live.

Not shut herself away from the world, but shine in it.

Of course, he would beg her to be with him first. She could shine with him. Failing that, he would let her shine alone. But dammit, she would shine. Scars and fears couldn't keep her hidden anymore.

She was beautiful. She deserved everything. And he had to make sure that she knew it.

"Why don't you go for a ride? Or a walk?"

Layna turned toward Mother Maria-Francesca, feeling distinctly ashamed just looking at the other woman. She shouldn't still be here taking up valuable space and sulking. Though, sulking seemed like too weak of a term.

"That's probably a good idea."

"Where will you go?" She detected a hint of concern in her voice. Probably afraid Layna would do something dire since she looked like a specter of death.

But she wouldn't. She couldn't honestly say she wouldn't. "Just up in the hills. To get a view of the ocean. My favorite place."

"Will you take Phineas?"

"No. I need the walk. I need to move slow. I have a lot of thinking to do."

She folded her arms beneath her breasts and walked out of the church building and out into the stormy weather. Wind was blowing in off the waves, rain threatening to fall from swollen gray clouds.

Layna lowered her head and started up the hill, not thinking, just feeling. Just letting her emotions wash through her.

She felt like she was drowning even while she was standing there breathing air. But the strangest thing was, she didn't feel like she was losing herself.

She scrambled to the top of a grass-covered hill and looked out over the ocean, tears blinding her. She hurt as much as she ever had, her heart smashed to pieces, shards embedded in her chest, but she wasn't fading into the mist.

Maybe it was because Xander's face was too strong in her mind. Maybe it was just because she had something, someone, to care about now.

Maybe it was because she finally knew who she was.

She wasn't a party girl with spoiled looks. Wasn't a princess who would never be crowned. She was Layna Xenakos, whatever her circumstances. Whatever her face. She was strong. She had run through hell and caught on fire along the way, left with scars that were inside and out, but she'd run through.

She had lost her faith, but for one blinding moment, she felt like maybe she'd found it.

Because this was that place again. That rock-bottom moment. But she wasn't alone.

She closed her eyes and tilted her face up to the sky, a raindrop landing on her cheeks. No, she wasn't alone. And she was strong.

A lump rose in her throat, a sob breaking through.

It didn't matter what happened. She could trust herself.

She could trust Xander.

Oh, Xander.

She needed to go to him. Because she loved him. Because he was the one she wanted to be with, that was the life she wanted.

She had to get down and beg for his forgiveness if that's what she needed to do. To ask him if he would take her, as she was, so broken and scared, when she'd been so horrible to him.

To tell him she feared nothing. Not pain, or love, or the media, more than she feared a lifetime without him.

She turned and her heart nearly stopped when she saw a dark head come into view, cresting the top of the hill, followed by a familiar face, and a heartbreakingly familiar body.

"Xander," she whispered.

And she ran to him.

Layna threw her arms around his neck and held him close to her, tears falling, her hands shaking. "What are you doing here?"

"I lied to you," he said, voice rough, his fingers forked through her hair, his face buried in her neck.

"You did?" she asked, pulling her head back so that she could look at him.

"I told you no more running. But I'm running now. To you."

She laughed as tears rolled down her cheeks. "Well, you're in luck because I just stopped running. So it looks like we're finally standing in the same place."

"It's about time," he said, kissing her lips. "It's about time."

"I love you," she said. "I was so scared, Xander. So scared to say it, or hear it, or feel it. But I found my faith. I found it and now I'm not afraid."

"I still can't give you your guarantee. Not as far as anything in life is concerned. But with me you have one. I'll always stand with you. I'll always stay with you. You will be my wife. The mother of my children. You're the only woman for me, Layna. Now and always. There are many uncertain things, but not my love."

"I don't need a guarantee. Not now. Faith is all about walking without sight. I don't need to see ahead, I just need to see you."

"You have no idea how glad I am to hear you say that."

She laughed. "About as glad as I am to say it?"

"I need to tell you this. I need you to understand—"

"I believe you, Xander, you have nothing to prove," she said, cupping his face and kissing him again. "I'm sorry I made you feel that you did. I'm sorry I doubted you. I'm sorry I let fear win. But it won't. Not again."

"But you need to hear this. I have walked down so many dark paths. I've chased pleasure in all its forms, and oblivion. I've tasted hopelessness. There was nothing there. No satisfaction. No answer. But with you, I find I am the man I'm meant to be. I find I'm the man I should have been all this time. You gave me the strength to face my father, to face this. I had to come and find you right away because somehow I knew I couldn't do it without you. I felt it."

She took a deep breath, of the sea and of Xander.

"I feel like we're standing at the beginning again. But better. Because I know so much more. I've been down those paths, too, and I know how dark they can be. So I know now just how important it is to always reach for the light. I know how weak I can be, but I also know how strong I can be."

"Very strong," he said. "You are so very strong."

"I wouldn't go back," she said, another tear spilling down her face. "I wouldn't take it back now. Because this is who I need to be. This is when we need to be. Not fifteen years ago when we would have made each other more vain and selfish, with equally vain and selfish children. But now."

"Now that I'm a broken-down playboy and you're a scarred novice? You are still only a novice, right? You didn't take vows, did you?"

"Nothing half so drastic, don't worry. But, yes, the scarred novice and the broken-down playboy with no pedigree. That's exactly who we needed to be."

"It was always going to be us in the end, wasn't it?" he asked.

She nodded. "I think so. How else would we survive all of this if we couldn't hold on to each other?"

"We wouldn't," he said. That simple. That certain.

"I'm just glad we got to become better versions of ourselves before it happened."

"I'm just glad that we're finally together."

"So am I."

"And we're together because of how much I love you, because of how much you love me. Not for Kyonos. Not for appearances. Not for any other reason."

He picked her up, and spun her in a circle, rain falling in earnest now, soaking them both. She flung her hands wide and let it fall on her, let it wash away the years. The regret. The pain. So all that remained was love.

"You know," she said, "I always felt the most free when I was riding my horse. But now I just feel that way. I just feel free."

"We both are, Layna. We both are."

EPILOGUE

Fifteen years later...

"HE'S GOING TO outlive us all." Xander sat down on the edge of the bed and looked at his wife. He was exhausted from the ball, a sort of "coming out" affair for Jessica and Stavros's oldest daughter. His own daughters had been so excited about it they'd been driving him mad for weeks.

Now they were feverishly planning their own, even though it was some years off. Mak and Eva's oldest son had reacted to the entire thing with the same sullenness of his father, and nothing his squealing cousins had done to entice excitement from him had worked. The same had been true for Xander and Layna's son, who had copied his cousin's practiced disdain. They had succeeded very well in annoying the girls, which Xander privately assumed was their goal.

He sighed. How he'd become the father of

two teenage girls and a sullen preteen boy he didn't know.

"Entirely possible," Layna said. She was standing by the vanity, all long elegant lines. He was always fascinated by the way she removed her jewelry. The way her fingers moved, the way she stood.

But then, everything Layna did fascinated him. Now and always.

"Can you believe the way he moves around the palace in that motorized cart of his? It's…well, it's the funniest thing I've ever seen."

King Stephanos had firmly denied both death and doctors and was a very crotchety old man. Xander was the acting ruler at this point, his father not able to perform most of the functions required by the position, but that didn't mean he wasn't still acting the figurehead. With gusto.

"It's that Drakos spirit," she said. "You're all too stubborn to be defeated."

He smiled. "True enough." Ever since that day he'd reconciled with his father he'd felt like a Drakos, unquestionably. "I still hate wearing ties to these things," he said, tugging the black scrap of silk off and letting it fall to the floor.

Layna smiled and walked over to him, planting her hands on the bed on either side of him, leaning down for a kiss. "The torture you're subjected to," she said, smiling that special smile of hers.

He kissed the crease by the corner of her mouth. "I know it."

"So tell me, Xander Drakos, heir to the throne, have you ever regretted coming back?"

"Not once. I would wear a tie every day of my life so long as I spent those days with you."

"Now that was the right answer."

"I'm getting pretty good at this husband thing."

"You've been good at it for a while," she said.

She kissed him again, deeper, more passionately. And then he was lost. As he always was with her. Years hadn't diminished their need for each other, their love.

Much, much later, Xander held his wife against his chest, threading his fingers through her hair, stroking her scar-roughened cheek.

"Layna Drakos, you make me very glad that I stopped running."

* * * * *

Mills & Boon® Large Print
July 2014